Booley and CC started down the street toward the Bucket O'Blood, us with them, and eleven snakes behind us. Ho, man, if Daddy saw me with that bunch I would be had-it for sure. *Had! It!*

We passed by the row of shops bright and crowded with tourists and sailors who had no idea what's about to go down.

Get the gun, get the gun, get the gun, I kept thinking.

Eleven jungle assassins and five of us must have made a powerful sight. You could see it in the scared faces watching us go by. Even the sailors were looking worried.

ALSO AVAILABLE IN LAUREL-LEAF BOOKS:

FOR ANDREW —

SHARK BAIT

GRAHAM SALISBURY

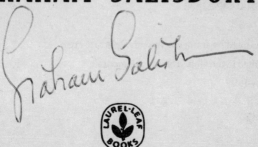

Published by
Bantam Doubleday Dell Books for Young Readers
a division of
Random House, Inc.
1540 Broadway
New York, New York 10036

Visit us on the Web! www.randomhouse.com

**Educators and librarians, for a variety of teaching tools,
visit us at www.randomhouse.com/teachers**

ISBN: 0-440-22803-4

RL: 4.6

Reprinted by arrangement with Delacorte Press

Printed in the United States of America

May 1999

10 9 8 7 6 5 4 3 2 1

OPM

For the young people of Hawaii.
Choose right.
Imua!

CHAPTER 1

Seven o'clock. Morningtime, last Saturday. Hot already. I was going out to swim in the ocean, and there he was with his shotgun. Had it pointed to the sky, sighting down the barrel.

"What'choo doing, Daddy?" I said.

"Morning, Eric. Going for your workout?"

"Yeah. What'choo got that gun out for?"

Click! He pulled the trigger. "Just checking it. Peace officer's gotta keep his equipment in good shape, you know. Never can tell when it will save his life."

"From what?"

Daddy shrugged. "You never know. Hey, you

1

heard anybody talking about a fight, somebody looking for revenge? Rumors going 'round."

"No," I told him. "What fight?"

"Never mind. You going down to see the Navy ship? Coming in today."

When he said *Navy*, I remembered—Booley Domingo. Yeah, Booley. He's the one who was looking to fight. Tonight. And that's one fight I was planning to see, man. Big as a truck, Booley, and only seventeen. But he looks older because of his size. Must be couple hundred pounds, maybe more. The most awesome part about him is his hair, all greased back to one short ponytail about three inches long. The guy look like Mafia.

I kept what I knew to myself. Booley Domingo was my friend and Daddy was Jimmy Chock, chief of police. "Yeah, I heard," was all I said.

"Well, you come home early today, okay?"

"Aw, man, how come?"

Just then Moms yelled down from the porch. "Daddy . . . telephone."

"Who is it?"

"Sergeant Tiumalu."

"Tell him I be right there."

Moms put her hand on her hip, frowning when she saw Daddy with that shotgun. She had on jeans and a blue work shirt with the sleeves cut off. Her eyes, blue as the shirt, said she didn't like that gun one little bit. Moms shook her head and went back inside the house, the screen door slapping.

"Okay, then," Daddy said, turning back to me. "Six o'clock, you be home. Going to be a lot to worry about when all those sailors get off that boat, and I don't want to worry about you too."

"Come on, Daddy, you don't have to worry about me. It's stupit to be home that early."

He just looked at me.

"Okay, okay . . . How's about ten o'clock, then? That's early."

"Six."

"Nine."

Daddy put his hand on my face. "I love you, son."

" *'Kay* then, six o'clock. Sheese."

He smiled and put that shotgun back in his car, then went inside to answer the phone.

Before I went out to swim, I slid behind the wheel of his car. Red Firebird with a bubble-light stuck on top. Hoo, every time I got in there I could feel the power. Like I was Daddy, driving around with that shotgun, police radio, handcuffs, searchlight, gun on my hip, flashing badge, fast car. Like having muscles. Pow! Don't mess with me. Someday I going be a cop too. Already Daddy's teaching me to shoot.

Yesterday him and Moms took me up to the dump to practice on soda cans with Uncle Randy's old Bulldog .38 police pistol. But before I could fire one shot I had to wait for Daddy to check around for cats. You see, even though Moms hates to see me shooting Daddy's guns, she hates worse that wild cats have to live at the dump, especially when they have kittens. Because of the mongooses, yeah? Which are like rats. Kittens don't last long around those things. So sometimes Moms comes to the dump with me and Daddy to see if there are any kittens there she can save.

No joke. True story.

So anyways, me and Moms sat watching on the trunk of Daddy's car while Daddy picked his way through steaming mountains of stink. "I thought I saw something move a little farther down there," Moms said, pointing deeper into the rising tide of rotting garbage.

Daddy scowled back at us and we laughed.

"Hurry it up, Daddy," I called. "I like shoot, already." He just waved me off, like, cool your jets.

So I waited, the .38 in my hand, smooth and heavy. I couldn't put any bullets in it until he got back.

It wasn't long.

I saw him freeze, his eyes pinned on a greasy cardboard box. He stepped closer and a cat came out of the box with its hair standing straight up. It had tiger-size fangs and claws that said *Get away from here before I scratch your eyeballs out and eat them.*

Daddy backed away.

"What is it?" Moms called.

"Crazy mother cat."

"She have any kittens in there?"

The cat watched Daddy, slowly crouching down, growling almost like a dog. It was so loud even I could hear it. Anyone could tell she had kittens in that box.

Daddy reached down and picked up a board and poked it at the mother cat to get her to move away. But instead she leaped toward him, batting at the board. Daddy jumped back. He looked like he was about to give up and walk away. Too much trouble.

"Oh, Jimmy, get them," Moms said in her sweetest voice. "We can't let them *die* out here."

Daddy frowned at Moms, and she said, "Pleeease."

Daddy shook his head and went back to poking the cat with the end of the wood. "Shoo! Go!" he said.

Fat chance.

The cat held her ground, slapping at the board and growling. Daddy moved closer. Looked like he was sword fighting with the cat. Finally, the cat gave a last hiss and took off.

"Eric," Daddy called. "Get the burlap sack from the trunk. And bring the socks."

Moms and I jumped off the trunk. I got the sack

5

and old sweat socks, and took them down into the dump, walking only on the toes of my thongs, like I was wading through six inches of barf, which wasn't far from the truth.

When I got there, I peeked down into the box and saw them: five gray-striped kittens, cowering in the farthest corner. Daddy took the socks and slipped them over his hands like gloves.

"Hold that bag open," he said.

Daddy reached in, slowly, then jerked his hand back out. "Tshaah! *Jeepers!*" he said. "Little rat bit me."

"Cat, Daddy," I said. "Those are cats."

Daddy gave me a stink look, then went back to work. Those kittens were as wild as their mother, I tell you. They scratched about two miles of skin off his hands, even with the socks on. But he got all five of them into the bag.

"I don't know why you do this, Daddy," I said. "They just going put them to sleep."

"Yeah, well, you tell your mother that. Anyway, sometimes people come adopt them." The Humane Society always rolled their eyes when they saw Daddy coming with some fresh batch of fleabite kittens. But they never complained. And you know, people did adopt some of them.

Moms was so happy with those kittens that she totally forgot to be worried about me and Daddy and Uncle Randy's .38.

"Okay," I said. "Now can I shoot?"

"Now you can shoot, son."

I fired off a whole box of bullets. Hit fourteen cans dead-on. Not bad. Daddy didn't touch the gun. Just sat there watching. Used to be was him and Uncle Randy who did the shooting. Both of them would bet money on targets, even though Daddy always ended up with fatter pockets. They liked to argue. That was their fun. Uncle Randy was a cop too, but a couple hundred miles away in Honolulu. He came to visit us about once a month, since he wasn't married. They were brothers, and friends too.

Then one day Uncle Randy put a kid in a wheelchair with that same gun, the .38. He missed the man he was shooting at and hit a boy. My uncle quit the force and moved to Kauai, became a farmer. Now he was about three hundred miles away.

I know I'm never supposed to touch that gun if Daddy's not around. But I can't help it, sometimes. That gun would be mine someday. Daddy said. He's starting to trust me with it, but he wasn't ready to give it up yet, not until he taught me to "respect" it. Sheese, I respected it already. The thing could take your head off in one shot. Daddy's always telling me guns are for protection or target practice, or hunting. "Guns are not toys, you got that, son?"

Yeah sure, but to me, when you got one of those things on your hip, people say "Yes officer, no officer, thank you sir, I sorry for speeding sir, I sorry for not wearing seat belt." Funny how some of my friends, especially Kalani Douglas, they got junk daddys—Kalani's is a mean drunk; Reggie's is never home. But my daddy is Jimmy Chock. I guess you could say I'm pretty lucky.

After a few minutes of fooling around in Daddy's police car I got out and went down to the rocks and jumped in the ocean. Nice, that water first thing. All summer I've been working out, getting ready for freshman football, coming up in a couple weeks. Me, Reggie, Kalani, and a bunch of other guys practiced all last year. No team. Just us. Someday we going play varsity at Konawaena High. I got a cousin, Keoni. You know him? Star fullback at Konawaena? One bull, man. He got a scholarship from San Jose State.

I swam out past the waves, way out. Deep water. Then I started working, swimming like I was one of those Olympics guys, getting the rhythm. I was trying to concentrate only on how my muscles were getting bigger, and how my endurance was getting stronger.

But I couldn't, because I had only one thought in my head: sharks. Cripes, I could be swimming alone like that, minding my own business, then *whop*, no more leg. All you got to do is be in the wrong place at the wrong time. What if there was a hungry white-tip looking for breakfast? Hoo, gave me chicken skin, I tell you, because even though Daddy is Chinese, I could be mistaken for a haole, a white person, and Booley said sharks drool for haoles. "For real, Mokes," he said. "Those things *love* white meat."

I looked around, checking for shark fins. Two days ago I saw one, gray and sharp as a machete. Then, *zip*—gone. *Spooky*, man.

Stop! Think rhythm, think endurance, think football. Think *anything*. Think Monica—yeah, *Monica*.

But still—*shark*.

Forget it, I told myself. No shark going eat you. Anyways, if I kept thinking like that I'd never swim in the ocean, yeah? And I would be laughed out of Kailua if I was chicken to swim in deep water. So I go out, way out. Every day.

I worked for an hour and a half, then dragged myself out, water streaming from my hair. I wiped my face with my hand and glanced up at the house. Moms was hugging Daddy goodbye near his car. Just as I looked, she screeched and jumped back. Daddy prob'ly tickled her. He always does that when she hugs him too long.

There was a small cardboard box on the grass and Daddy picked it up. The kittens from the dump. Daddy put the box in his car and got in and started it. He looked out at Moms and stuck out his hand. Moms grabbed it and held on as he started to drive away, then let go.

9

I looked back at the ocean, all clean and blue and quiet as a full-up rain barrel. What a day.

Then I remembered: *Be home at six.*

I kicked the sand and walked back up to the house thinking about the promise I didn't want to keep.

CHAPTER 2

I took a shower from the hose on the grass and went inside. Already Moms was doing housework, wiping salt spray from the surf off everything so nothing would rot or corrode. She always does that first, every day. Then she goes out to her shed behind the house and works for about ten hours making bowls, plates, cups, and vases out of clay. Nice, what she makes. She sells them in hotel shops.

"Have a good swim?" Moms said, and I said, "Yeah, real good," on my way to put on a T-shirt and shorts.

My room smelled like bacon from Daddy's breakfast. Moms always cooks up something nice for him. Treats him like a king. But that's how it should be, because there's nobody like Daddy. Tough as an eel, sure, but if you give him respect he'll give it back. Even to me and my friends, not just to Moms and his own friends.

Whap! I punched my hand. *Six o'clock.* Shhh. Daddy told me more than once: "Always keep your word, Eric. A man's got nothing if he hasn't got integrity." Ca-ripes. What I going do now?

Forget it. Worry about that later.

When Moms wasn't looking I went into Daddy's closet and got out Uncle Randy's .38. I took it to my room to clean it, because of yesterday when I shot it at the dump. Daddy kept it in a soft chamois, wrapped up with a box of bullets. I put the bullets on my desk and held the gun in my hand, running my fingers along the smooth, police-blue steel barrel. So, so *nice.* Six-shot single-action, walnut hand-checkered grip inlaid with abalone shells in the pattern of a snake.

But holding that gun made me kind of sad, too, because I hardly ever saw Uncle Randy anymore.

Just then I heard Reggie calling me from outside. "Mokes! Let's go. Past nine, already." Booley gave me that name, Mokes. Means tough guy. He was joking, yeah? Teasing me. But that's okay because I like Booley. And I know something about him that nobody knows but me.

"Hey, Mokes!" Reggie yelled through the window screen.

I hid the gun and the box of bullets under a dirty T-shirt on my desk. I'd finish cleaning it later. "Moms," I called. "I going down Kalani's house with Reggie."

Me, Reggie, and Kalani had plans to go check out the Navy ship, maybe take a ride on the launch, if they let people go aboard this time. The Navy came in about once a year. Usually they came on a buoy tender, or a minesweeper. Those things are so big they have to anchor way out in the bay. And sometimes they had guns on them too.

When this town smells those Navy guys coming, the police get ready. All day they have to cruise, back and forth, back and forth, watching everything, even if we only got three police—Daddy, Sergeant Tiumalu, and Rocky Machado. People gotta feel safe. Around here, those Navy swabbys ain't got a very good rep. They swarm all over the place, drinking and making noise and chasing after everybody's wife and girlfriend. Not to mention breaking a couple windows, every time. None of those cops would be home until tomorrow morning.

The Navy got cops too. They call them SP for Shore Patrol, or Sea Police, or Sweety Pies, I don't know. But those SP guys don't fool around. One time I saw them drag a sailor back to the ship because he was drinking too much and making problems around town. If it was Daddy, he would just try to talk the guy down, give him a break. Daddy always says you should try "verbal persuasion" first.

But those SP guys cracked that swabby with their sticks. *Bok! Bok!*

"Swabby"—that's what we call them. Or sometimes we call them milk bottles, because they so white, yeah? in those uniforms.

"Mokes, let's go!" Reggie called. "You still sleeping, or what?"

"All right, all right, I'm coming." Reggie drove me crazy sometimes. He was always moving, bouncing his nervous leg when he sat, slapping drum sounds on his knees, sticking his hand in his armpit and making fut sounds. Sheese. But Reggie was a good guy, most of the time. He had one of those tight, muscled bodies with absolutely no fat. Filipino. And he was a killer quarterback. He and Kalani were my best friends.

Before I got two steps past the door Moms poked her face out the window. "Remember, Daddy said to be home by six."

"Yeah, I know."

"Don't forget, now, Eric."

When we were halfway up to the road, Reggie said, "How come you gotta be home at six?"

"Because of the Navy guys."

"What about them?"

"Ca-ripes, I don't know. My parents worry about everything."

Reggie shook his head. "Too bad, man. You going miss the fight."

"What'choo mean miss it?"

"Well, Booley prob'ly ain't going fight till night-time, and you, being one daddy's boy, you going be home when he says."

"Shuddup." I shoved Reggie.

He laughed, the stupit. Kalani was the one who started calling me that. Makes me so mad. All because one time he wanted me to loan him my knife, a World War II one my uncle Randy gave me. "Can't," I told him. "My daddy said don't let it out." Kalani said, "You one daddy's boy, or what?"

"Daddy's boy," Reggie said again, and I grabbed his T-shirt with both hands. "Hey, hey, hold on, Mokes. Relax, already."

I looked in his eyes with all the murder I could. Then I pushed him away. "I ain't! No! *Daddy's* boy!"

Reggie stumbled back, saying, "O-*kay*. *Sorry*." Then he grinned.

I scowled at my feet as we walked down to Kalani's house. The road was already so hot you could make footprints in the soft tar. I made like I was all mad at Reggie, but inside I wasn't. In that place it was cool that he pushed me, because it gave me a chance to push back. I had to live up to my name: *Tough Guy*.

CHAPTER 3

Kalani's yard was dead quiet.

Except for Bozo, who was tied up on the porch. When that lolo mutt saw us coming he jumped up and started barking like we were Frankenstein and Godzilla. He leaped at us, straining the rope and snarling and snapping and choking himself, and all I can say is that dog should be in a dog insane asylum. Bozo. Good name.

Kalani likes dogs. He's got three. One is Eddy, deaf and old as dried-up bones. Kalani found him shaking in the bushes with a bullet hole in his leg. Boy, was Kalani mad. How could somebody shoot a dog? He took him home.

17

And then Kalani's brother, James, who lives in Hilo now, gave him a puppy, one ant-size dogette. Part Chihuahua, or something ridiculous like that, a nervous mutt that makes shi-shi on your feet every time he comes by you. Man, that little flea gets *excited*. Kalani calls him Spike. Those mangy mutts are his family, since his moms is dead, his brother ran away, and his daddy is crazy.

"Hey, Kalani," I called from the yard.

No way I was going any closer with Bozo showing those yellow fangs.

"Kalani!"

"Bead it," somebody shouted from inside the dark house. "Ged oudda my yard."

Mr. Douglas, Kalani's old man.

His face scowled through the screen door. He had on boxer underwear, and his hair stood up like a hurricane. He scratched his fat belly. "He not he', tho bead it, b'fore I lit dith dog eat-thoo."

"What?" It's hard to understand somebody when they're missing half their teeth. "I looking for Kalani," I said.

"Not 'ome, bead it!"

"Where he went?" I asked.

Kalani's daddy came outside, pushing open the screen door, squeaking on the rusty hinge. He glared at me. He knows my daddy. Those two met up plenty times, and Mr. Douglas don't let me forget it.

He started coughing, harder and harder, until he

bent over and put his hands on his knees. All the time Bozo was leaping at us, shaking his wild-eyed head, strangling himself on his rope.

Me and Reggie got out of there.

Down at the harbor, the bay was glassy and quiet. I could only see two, three tourists walking around out on the pier. Our town was pretty small. It was a fishing town, and a tourist town too. A long seawall curved around the edge of the harbor. We had one street with low buildings. It was a peaceful place, and sometimes pretty boring. But not today.

We found Kalani sitting on the seawall, fishing with a bamboo pole. He saw us coming and raised his chin, *hey*. Kalani was the good-looking one of us guys. Girls went crazy for him, that sly smile and Portuguese-Hawaiian skin and a cool scar that ran across one of his eyebrows. He was six feet, almost, and built like a cane truck from canoe paddling. He had a friendly, calm way about him that you had to like. A true friend.

"Hey, Kalani," I said, walking up. "You got to put that lolo Bozo to sleep, man. Someday he going eat somebody."

Kalani tapped his hand on the concrete. "Sit, punks. From here we got a front-row seat for the Navy. I heard they coming around noontime. A destroyer."

The sun was frying the back of my neck, so I took

off my T-shirt and made an Arab hat around my head and let half of it hang down my back.

Kalani hauled up a five-inch hinalea, shaking and flashing wet in the sun. He grabbed the flipping fish and gently took out the hook.

"Why you catching hinalea?" I said. "You can't eat that."

"That's his ancestor. His aumakua," Reggie said. "They having a family reunion."

"Shuddup," Kalani said, dropping the fish back in the water. "Don't make fun of aumakua, Reggie. They help you, you know. They take care of their descendants. Their good ones, anyway." Kalani grinned. "Which means you in trouble, brah."

"Hinalea is your aumakua, Kalani?" I asked.

"True fact, Mokes," Reggie said. "His spirit ancestors are all junk fish. That one he just dropped was his great-granma reminding him to eat all his vegetables."

Kalani slugged Reggie's arm. "Going be one ta-riffic day, today. I can smell it. Navy guys going come and Booley going fight and it don't get *noooo* better than that."

The last time a Navy ship came in, Booley Domingo picked a fight with a haole swabby. Booley hates, hates, *hates* white Navy guys, because his moms ran off with one about four years ago. She met him in a hotel bar. One month after that sailor's ship left, Booley's moms was gone. *Poof.* Busted up the family, and busted up Booley. He took it hard. Like I said, I know something about him that nobody else does.

When my moms heard about Mrs. Domingo running off, she said to Daddy, "It was bound to happen, you know, Jimmy. She was a very unhappy woman." And Daddy said, "Yeah, and now I know a very unhappy man." I was thinking, Yeah, sure, but what about Booley? What about his sister, who was just a baby? I felt bad for them. So did Kalani and Reggie.

But anyways, the last time a Navy ship came, Booley went looking for a fight and found one with a big swabby, a monster guy with a square jaw and small eyes. Not a good choice. Booley ate it right in front of all us guys and half the town. The Navy guy just chewed him up and spit him out. And when he walked away, Booley said, "I going *kill* you!" Luckily, the SPs grabbed the guy and took him back to the ship.

But now Booley was bigger. And stronger.

Just as I was thinking that, Booley and his scary friend CC drove by with their car radio thumping ghetto bass.

Booley's car was a primer-gray low-rider, a chopped and beefed-up Cadillac with two extra-fat tires in the back, its star-shaped rims flashing in the sun. *Noisy*, that car, because Booley took off the muffler. He'd cut the windows and the roof down to almost half and made low seats, so when he drove it you could only see half his face, his eyes, and that Mafia hair. He looked cool driving so slow, so smooth.

Ho, *yeah*, I was thinking. Now it begins. Booley would take his revenge today. Just please, please, *please* let it be before six o'clock.

Booley saw us and lifted his chin, Howzit, punks. He could almost be Kalani's brother, they looked so alike. Both mostly Hawaiian, and both big.

Booley looked at me and grinned. "Shark Bait," he said.

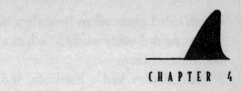

CHAPTER 4

Booley turned up his radio even more, then headed toward the pier.

His friend CC, sitting in that car with tattoos wrapped around his biceps like armbands, gave us burning stink eye. He had a shaved head and a frown on his face that never took a break. He and Booley had been friends since about first grade. Kalani told me CC was number nine in a family of thirteen kids, all wild, except for one girl who never yet in her life has said one word.

None of us knew why, but CC always sat in the backseat of Booley's car. Weird. Reggie said for sure not all that guy's dogs was barking. CC started to go bad in third grade when he stole a bike from some-body's yard. Daddy said CC's had a hard life for a boy of seventeen.

Well, Booley had a hard life, too, starting from when his moms ran. Sometimes Booley was nice. But sometimes bombs went off in his head, and *boom*, watch out. "Be careful with that boy," Daddy said, even though he liked Booley. "He wants to do the right thing, Eric, but it's hard for him."

Booley worked on the *Captain Cook*, the tourist boat his daddy used to skipper, the one that takes people down the coast to where Captain Cook was killed. I liked Booley, and, well, I guess you could say I owed him. You see, it was him who gave me a life in this town.

About five years ago, when I first came here, I had a hard time making friends. I was only in fourth grade, and we'd just moved over from Honolulu be-cause of Daddy's police chief job. I was the only white kid for a thousand miles in any direction, it felt like. But the funny thing is, I wasn't really white. I had a little bit of Hawaiian and a lot of Chinese, too. Everybody wondered how I could look so haole . . . until they saw my moms, who was as white as ice cream.

But anyways, I used to hang out on the seawall by myself, missing my Honolulu friends and watching the deep-sea charter fishing boats come and go. It was kind of a lonely time, and so, so boring.

But not always.

There were days when this small gang of creeps came to town, from where I didn't know. At first they didn't say a word to me, but man, did they give me eye. I tried not to look at them, but it was hard. They were older, maybe sixth grade.

One day I was on the seawall and I met this little girl. She was only about two years old and she was wandering around by herself. She had no fear of falling off into the water, and no fear of strangers. It seemed like nobody was watching out for her.

Well, she walked up and sat down next to me. "Are you fishing?" she asked.

I looked at her, thinking, Whoa, this kid sounds pretty grown up already. "No," I said.

"I'm Sissy."

I reached out to shake her hand and said, "I'm Eric."

She smiled when we shook, and it made me feel so good. I liked her.

I didn't know it then, but across the bay a guy was watching us through binoculars from the *Captain Cook*. And the guy was her brother—Booley Domingo.

One day those sixth-grade punks came up to me when I was sitting on the seawall talking with Sissy. There were four of them, mean and cold. "Eh, boy," one guy said, looking down at me. "Get up."

I stood up, and thought I would faint.

The four of them snickered, like, look how they could make me jump up. Good boy, good dog. "We don't like you," the boy said.

"What?"

Then he spit on me, hit me in the chest, and waited for me to do something about it.

Just then Booley came up behind them. He was a couple years older than those punk guys. The kid who spit on me didn't see him until it was too late. Booley grabbed him and threw him into the ocean. Ho, man, *boom!* The guy's swimming.

The other punks ran.

Booley said to me, "Better take off that shirt before it rots on you."

I did, the guy's spit and my own trembling stomach making me feel sick.

"You the cop's kid, yeah? Your daddy's the new chief. Chief Chock."

I nodded and said, "Thanks for—"

"Lissen, boy, you nothing but shark bait in this town. One white kid like you ain't going last long, at least if you not tough. You tough enough?"

I shrugged.

Booley smiled. "No worry. You been nice to Sissy, so I going make you tough enough. How's about that?"

I grinned.

"Man, you look like a squid," he said after I got

the shirt off. "How come you get Chinese last name and you so white?"

"Only about half Chinese. The other half is Swedish."

Booley made a smirk-face. "*Swedish*? No wonder those punks like feed on you. But forget that. Hey, you like come out on the boat sometime?"

"Yeah," I said. "Really?"

"How's about next week?"

"Yeah, sounds g—"

"Lissen, Shark Bait. I going tell you three things you gotta know to live in this town. You ready?"

"Yeah!"

"Good. Okay. Number one: You got friends, you stand by them. They got trouble, then you got trouble. Like the musketeers, yeah? One for all, and all for one. Okay, number two is you don't rat on *nobody*, got it? I don't care who it is. And number three is you don't let nobody shame you, no matter if they grind your face in the dirt. You get up, and you come back, and you face them till you drop. Then, even if you lose, you still got respect. If you can do those three things, then you going be tough enough for this town. Got that?"

"Y-Yeah, but . . ."

"Good. So how's about I buy you and Sissy one ice cream? Come, Sissy, we go store."

So you see, Booley was okay.

27

The next week, Daddy drove me down to the pier to the *Captain Cook*. Booley and five other guys were already working like ants, cleaning and polishing and joking around, getting the boat ready for the tourists. Booley shook hands with me and Daddy.

"So come meet the guys," Booley said after Daddy left. He put his arm on my shoulder, and it felt good. "You guys be nice to this mokes, yeah?" Booley told the other deckhands. "This kid's my friend." The guys gave me Cokes, showed me how to tie a rolling hitch, a clove hitch, and a bowline, stuff like that, all the time saying things like, "How's it going, Mokes?" and "Hey, Mokes, you pretty good with those knots," and on that day I knew I would love this town.

After a while a bus drove out onto the pier. "Look," Booley said. "Here come the cows."

The bus groaned to a stop, brakes hissing. "Here we go, brah," he said, then jogged over to help the tourists up the boarding ramp.

The ocean was easy and smooth all the way down the coast to Kealakekua Bay, where Captain Cook's monument was, which was what all those tourists came to see.

The bay was kind of a paradise, deep-water green and glassy. A straight-up cliff with caves in it rose from the ocean. Above that was jungle. On the left side of the cliff the land curled down into trees and bushes that spread out flat to the ocean's edge.

The boat slowed as it circled into the cove. Booley came over and stood next to me at the rail. "Nice, yeah?"

"What do you do here?"

"Take the small boat to shore, look around." He nodded toward the monument, a white spike-like thing surrounded by trees. Nothing else was there, no people, no houses. "That's where they killed Captain Cook. Smashed his head in with rocks."

Booley left to help drop anchor. He came back and said, "You can come on the small boat, or go diving, check out the fish. You got about an hour. But watch out for sharks, yeah?" He flicked his eyebrows up and down.

"What? Sharks . . . here?"

"Sure."

"You lie."

"Try see."

The tourists crowded around the rail, ready to go ashore. "I gotta go," Booley said. "Listen for snapping teeth, yeah?"

Forget the monument. Who wanted to see where somebody died? I checked the water. No sharks. No deep shadows. I figured he was joking and dove off the bow.

The water was cold. And deep.

I swam toward the cliff, where huge boulders had broken away and crashed down into the sea. I stumbled out of the water onto them, and found a spot where I could lie like a lizard in the sun.

The heat off the rocks instantly warmed my skin.

Across the bay I could see the tourists poking around in the bushes near the monument. I turned and looked up at the cliff. How come it had all those holes in it? I tried to climb up and check one out.

It was too steep, but I did find a piece of old bone, bleached white and splintery. Ho! Maybe it was human. I stuck it in my pocket and swam back to the *Captain Cook*.

When I showed it to Booley, he jumped away and said, "*Yahhh!* Take that thing back!"

"Why?"

"Just take it back! Now! Take it where you found it!"

"But—"

"Go!"

I stuck the bone in my pocket and dove overboard. What was he so cranked up about?

I put the bone back where I found it and got out of there.

Booley stayed away from me on the way back. He looked nervous. Just before we got to the harbor he came over. "Lissen," he said, almost whispering. "I telling you, boy . . . you *never* mess with old bones. I mean it. It happened to me.

"One time, down by my house, I found a cave. I

went inside and looked around. I found this old dried-up human skull and took it home. I liked it. Kind of spooky. I didn't tell nobody about it. That night, I went to sleep and woke up just after midnight with wind blowing over my sheets like a hurricane, making all kind rattling sounds. *Spooky*, I tell you. But not only that, I had this pressure on my chest. *Man*, it was heavy, like somebody was sitting on me. Pushing down, hard. I couldn't breathe. But nobody was there. What it was, I don't know, but it was real, I tell you, and it had something to do with that skull. I said, *Okay, okay, I'll take it back*, and *boom!* the wind stopped and the pressure left. My hands were shaking and I had sweat all over me. The next morning, before the sun came up, I took it back and never messed with bones again. I telling you this for your own good.''

I stared at him. Was he teasing me, like the shark thing? He looked scared.

''Those holes in the cliff are old Hawaiian burial caves,'' he said. ''That bone came from there, prob'ly. Maybe a bird took it out, I don't know. But no matter how it got out, don't ever mess with dead bones. Dead peoples don't like it.''

My palms started to sweat. I rubbed them on my shorts.

Booley put his hand on my shoulder. ''S'okay, boy. You didn't know. But now you do, yeah?''

A year later, after me and Reggie became friends, I told him that story. He crossed himself like you do before you go in the ocean. "He saved your life, Mokes. I'm not kidding. If you hadn't put that bone back, you would be cursed. Or dead. Or cursed *and* dead."

CHAPTER 5

So Booley drove by me, Reggie, and Kalani and went out on the pier and parked. We watched from the seawall, waiting for him to get out of his car. But he and CC just sat there.

A few minutes later trouble came driving by.

Leonard Biao, the jungle-boy criminal, him and his friends.

You see, on this side of the island we had two groups, mountain guys and ocean guys, and the two didn't mix. It was them and us. That's just the way it was. But at the moment, we had a kind of truce. Nobody was looking for a fight.

They came in two cars. Leonard, a mean

eleventh-grade junior convict who everybody knew Booley hated, was driving the first one. Both cars were packed with mountain guys. I didn't want to be within a hundred miles of them.

Leonard saw us on the seawall and stopped. His left arm hung out the window, and I could see the one half-missing finger on his hand.

His fake smile flashed *danger*. "Try come," he said.

None of us moved.

"Try *come*," he said again, and we jumped down off the wall.

"What?" Reggie said.

Leonard, with one shiny silver front tooth gleaming, gave something to Reggie.

"What's this?" Reggie said, but all of us knew exactly what that rolled-up white thing was. Daddy was always telling me to watch out for guys like him, who try to give you paka or speed or whatever kind of drugs and try to hook you, then milk you for all you got later on. "That stuff will ruin your life," Daddy said. "If you're ever going to listen to me, listen now. That stuff is bad." I told him I would *never* mess with it, and he said, "Every day I pray for that, son."

"Primo, that one," Leonard said to Reggie. "On the house. You know who to call when you like more, yeah? Make you folks a good deal." He flashed his piranha smile one last time, then put his car in gear and cruised out to the pier.

"Throw it away," Kalani said to Reggie. "It's nothing but trouble."

"It's Leonard Biao who's nothing but trouble," I said.

Reggie ran the weed under his nose. "Smells like the real thing, all right."

"How do *you* know?" I said.

"My sister, Janet. She had some. Smell just like this."

None of us guys had ever smoked that stuff. That I knew of, anyway. But for sure not me.

Leonard parked on the pier like Booley, and like Booley, he stayed in his car. From what I could see Leonard didn't look at Booley, and Booley didn't look at him. But had to be they were checking each other out.

"Man, I hate to see those guys in this town."

"They smell action," Kalani said.

"Yeah, Booley's action."

"If Booley looks bad tonight," Kalani said, "then Leonard going crown himself king."

That thought—Leonard Biao as king around this place—made me squirm.

About noontime a long, gray destroyer cruised into the bay from the north, came steaming around the point and was suddenly there. It anchored way out, so big it made our harbor look like a rain puddle. That thing stood out like a bloody eye.

For a long time it just sat there.

Except for a couple of fish that jumped in the harbor, nothing moved.

Finally the Navy dropped a launch.

When the launch was about halfway to the pier, Booley started up his car. *Varoom! Vaarooooom!* He cruised away.

Reggie shook his head. "I hope that guy who shamed him ain't on that boat."

"No way." I spit. "Booley never going see him again."

"Then I hate to be the guy who going take his place."

"Mokes, look," Kalani whispered. "Here comes your sweetheart."

Just down from where we sat on the seawall there was a new bar made to look like an old-time grass shack. They called it the Bucket O' Blood Saloon. An Olympia beer truck had just pulled up in front of it. And walking past that truck was Reggie's sister, Janet. And with her, Monica.

"Hey, Monica!" Kalani yelled. "Mokes loves you!"

"Yahhhh," I said, clamping my hand over his mouth. "What if CC heard that?"

Monica just kept looking straight ahead like we

36

were some kind of rotten fish. Hoo, I like that Monica. So nice, so classy. Arms with nice shapes because she lifts weights, just like us guys. Reggie saw. He said she curls twenty-pound dumbbells. And not only that, her teeth are so white it makes you squint. She could be a lipstick model. Man, she makes me sweat and shake and mumble like I half lolo when she smiles at me. Which ain't often. Since fifth grade, already, I've had eyes for her.

But Monica going be eleventh grade. To her, I'm somebody's dog.

Anyways, that stupit Kalani could get me killed calling to her like that.

For me, this whole thing with Monica had a couple of big problems. Number one is I'm not Japanese. Monica is pure Japanese, which means forget it, because her parents like for her to hang out with only Japanese guys. Monica don't care about that, but the papa and mama do. Old country, yeah?

But worse than that—far worse—is number two: CC. He thinks Monica is *his*. Gotta be kidding. Reggie says Janet says Monica's scared to tell him to take a walk. At first Monica did like CC. When she found out he was so "jealous and possessive," she tried to back out of it. But she couldn't. CC wouldn't let her. Even if she could, then what? If CC catches anyone anywheres *near* Monica, it would be checkout time for that guy, and you better believe it, because CC already got arrested seventeen times. I heard that from Daddy, but he wouldn't tell me what CC did all those times, only that he was on probation and would most likely stay on probation until he was eighteen.

One of those times when CC was arrested Booley was with him and got arrested too. Prowling around Monica's house, throwing rocks on the roof.

But CC's not *all* bad. Booley told me one time he and CC were drinking and riding around in Booley's car, and CC busted off Mr. Fujikawa's mailbox with a crowbar. Next day CC felt real bad about it, because he liked Mr. Fujikawa, an old guy who never bothered anybody. So CC bought him a new mailbox and put it up himself.

So anyways, Monica and Janet walked by. Janet waved. But Monica didn't even glance at us. Kalani poked me with his elbow, then kissed his fingertips. "Aahhhhh," he whispered, grinning at me.

Back at the Bucket O' Blood I saw Daddy's police car pull up behind the Oly truck. He got out, hitched up his pants, then looked out at the destroyer. Kalani's cousin Robert the bouncer came out of the saloon to help the beer guy unload. When he saw Daddy he went over to talk, so us guys decided to go over and see what was going on.

Daddy saw us coming and smiled. "Look at these boys, Robert. Almost men already."

Robert said, "Scary, yeah, how fast they grow."

Daddy put his hand on my shoulder. "I'm a lucky

man, Robert. This boy of mine is going to make a fine peace officer someday." I looked down at my feet, trying to hide a grin.

Robert shook hands with us guys, macho-man style, and asked Kalani how his father was doing, but of course he prob'ly already knew because he had to see that drunk boozing it up in the Bucket O' Blood about every hour of every day.

"Still alive," Kalani said.

Robert nodded, then looked down. "Yeah, well, gotta get this truck unloaded," he said, and went to help the beer guy.

"Wait a minute," Daddy said. Daddy opened the back door of his car and came out with one of the dump kittens. "How about a cat?" he said to Robert. The kittens were pretty tame now.

Robert took the kitten, ran his hand down its back, scratched its head, considering. "Why not?" he said, and stuck the kitten in his shirt pocket. It fit, only its head poking out. Robert left to supervise the truck guy. I figured Robert must have had six cats by now.

"Hey," Daddy said to us. "I got a Navy joke. You boys want to hear it?"

"Sure," Reggie and Kalani said at the same time.

"Okay. Actually, this is not a joke. This really happened. There was this Navy captain on the ship radio, yeah? He says to this other ship he sees on his radar, *Please change your course ten degrees to the*

39

south to avoid a collision. And then a voice from the other guy comes back on the radio, *Recommend you change* YOUR *course ten degrees to the north to avoid a collision*. The Navy captain is getting angry now, says, *This is the captain of a U.S. Navy ship. I say again, divert your course*. Then the other guy comes back, *No, I say again, divert* YOUR *course*. Hoo, now the Navy guy is mad as can be, yeah? He says, *This is the aircraft carrier U.S.S.* Enterprise. *We are a large warship of the U.S. Navy. Divert your course* NOW. The other guy was silent a moment. Then he says, *This is a lighthouse. Your call."*

"*Aahhhhhahaha,*" us guys went. Crack us up, man, *this is a lighthouse*.

"That's good, Chief," Kalani said. "Where you heard that?"

"True story. Read it in the paper. Hey, I gotta go. Eric, keep your eyes open today. Practice seeing things most people don't notice—guys hanging around looking jumpy, strange cars in town, things like that. When you go to the police academy you'll be way ahead, already."

I nodded, and Daddy tapped my shoulder good-bye.

"Wait, can I take a kitten too?" I asked.

"What you got in mind, son?"

"Present for someone."

Daddy shrugged and let me pick one out of the box. I chose the fuzziest one in there.

"Remember when you're coming home, now."

"Yeah." *Ca-ripes,* I thought as Daddy got in his car and drove away. How come I made that promise to him? All I wanted for today was to have a good time with my friends and see Booley beef with some sailors.

I must have looked angry, because Reggie said, "What?"

"Nothing . . . only maybe I ain't gonna see Booley fight."

"How come?" Kalani said.

"I said *maybe.*"

Kalani shrugged. "Who you going give that flea-bite to?"

"Somebody."

"Hey, let's go Granma's place," Reggie said. "Borrow some cash. Maybe we can get a six-pack for tonight."

"Sounds good," Kalani said. Booley would buy it for you, if you paid him double.

But what about what I promised Daddy? Good boy. Good dog.

CHAPTER 6

Reggie's granma's barbershop was on a back street, up behind the Bucket O' Blood. Half barbershop, half house. We called it a babashop. Easy to say, like that. Anyways, that's what Granma called it. She lived there with Sissy, who was six years old now, and just about as smart as fourth or fifth grade. She could even cut hair. I let her cut mines once. Came out pretty good.

But the thing was, Sissy wasn't so lucky.

First, her and Booley's moms ran away. But what came after that was worse. Their daddy died about a year later. Booley took it hard, real hard. He was close to his daddy. After the daddy died Booley went to live with CC's family, and Sissy went to live with Granma, who isn't her real granma, but some kind of relative.

Moms said Mr. Domingo died of a broken heart. But Booley and Reggie know different. Reggie's uncle was with Booley's old man the night he died.

This is what happened.

One day Reggie's uncle and Booley's daddy went shore fishing. They hiked down the coast past Keauhou, down over the old lava flow. They were going to camp down there for the weekend. Reggie's uncle said they set up a tent and fished off the rocks until it got dark. Booley's daddy had a kerosene lamp and wanted to stay and night fish awhile. So Reggie's uncle stayed too.

Until he saw the lights.

Torches, it looked like, bobbing in the night.

Reggie's uncle got nervous, then scared. Booley's old man said it was just other fishermen, but Reggie's uncle was sure it was obake, ghosts.

It was Night Marchers, Reggie's uncle told Reggie. No way it was regular obake, not there. They were down near the old Hawaiian battlefield. Kuamo'o. Gave me the creeps, listening to Reggie tell it, because in school we learned about that place, about how it was where they had the bloodiest fight in the history of these islands. It was the first time Hawaiians used guns.

Anyways, you didn't mess with Night Marchers.

They weren't like regular ghosts. Booley told me about them. You see, inside us we got this spirit, called uhane, the thing that makes us move around. At night, when you are sleeping, your uhane can come out through the spirit hole in the corner of your eye. It goes out and talks with your aumakua, your ancestor protectors, to get advice, then comes back in your body before you wake up.

But when you die, your uhane, if you were good in life, goes to the heavenly underworld, a good place. If you were bad, then your uhane becomes an obake, or ghost, and it just wanders around on earth like it's lost. And it looks just like you looked when you were alive, except for one thing: no feet. It floats around and eats spiders and moths and scares you.

Anyway, Reggie said Night Marchers are different from those ghosts. They're the spirits of the old, old Hawaiians—the chiefs, the warriors, the priests and priestesses, like that. These ones are powerful. If at night you see them marching, and if they catch you, then they could kill you.

Reggie said, "My uncle saw the torches bobbing, a long line of them. They had this wild glow, like nothing real." Reggie looked nervous. He's scared to death of ghosts from when he was a small kid and his grampa used to tell him ghost stories before bed. "My uncle got out of there fast. He begged Booley's old man to run for it too, but Booley's daddy said, 'Forget it, I'm not bothering nobody.'"

Even Booley's daddy had heard that if they were Night Marchers, and they saw him, they'd kill him. No question, unless friendly aumakua were among the marchers and saved him. If not, one of the guards in front or in back of the marchers would kill him. *Poof!* Sometimes you heard a drum, or a flute. Sometimes they passed in silence. But Booley's daddy didn't care. He didn't believe in ghosts.

Reggie said, "So Booley's old man told my uncle he was being ridiculous. Those torches were just fishermen walking over the rocks." But Reggie's uncle ran for his life.

The next morning he went to look for Booley's old man, who never came back to the camp. He found him dead, still sitting there holding his fishing pole. "His heart just stopped," the coroner told the police.

"But don't you believe it, Mokes," Reggie said. "It was Night Marchers."

So now Sissy, with no moms and no daddy, lives with Granma, her closest relative. It's island blood that binds everyone together—Hawaiian, Filipino, Japanese, Chinese, all kind of mixed up. Reggie, Kalani, CC, and maybe even me, we could all prob'ly find some distant relation to Sissy.

But the best thing Sissy had going for her was her

brother. Booley would do anything for that little girl.

"Come, come," Granma said when we got to the babashop, waving us in, laughing like we were the Three Stooges walking up. "What'choo boys up to?"

"Nothing, Granma," Reggie said. "How's business?"

"Oh, liddie bit, liddie bit. Same like always."

"Hey, Sissy, gimme five," I said, and Sissy, smiling like crazy, came over and slapped me a good one. I made like it hurt like fire, shook my hand, and she laughed. Usually I bring her stuff like Pez or crack seed or Starburst. But this time I had something better. I pulled the kitten out from behind my back.

Ho, *man*, did her eyes pop. "A kitten! Granma, look what Mokes has."

"It's for you," I said, and Sissy covered her mouth with her hand.

Granma came over. "Oh, so *cute*."

Sissy gave me a big hug and took the kitten, which filled her little hands. She snuggled it against her cheek.

"You gotta take it to the vet and get it some shots," I said.

"What you going call it?" Kalani asked Sissy.

Sissy thought a minute. "Mokeyboy. After you, Mokes."

"Nah. Anyways, it's a girl. Call it Jeepers," I said, remembering how Daddy yelped when one of those kittens bit him at the dump.

"*Jeepers?*" Kalani said, making a gotta-be-kidding face.

"Private joke."

"Jeepers," Sissy whispered. "Let's go get some milk for you. Come on, Jeepers, then I'll show you your new home."

Her face was all happy, and Granma's too. Those two got their own little family. Booley tells everybody, "Get your hair cut at Granma's place." *Or die*, we all thinking. So Granma's pretty busy.

"Hey, Reggie," Granma said. "I saw you boys pissing on the seawall today. What'choo caught?"

"*Aaaaaaaa!*" We busted out laughing, holding our sides, almost crying. *I saw you pissing.* Granma cannot say *fishing*, cannot say *f* and *sh* on that old-time Filipino tongue. So *funny*.

"Hey, Granma," Reggie said, still laughing. "How's about I can borrow couple bucks?"

Granma went to the money drawer and gave him two dollars without even asking why. "Thanks," Reggie said. "I'll pay you back next week."

If Reggie says *borrow*, then he'll pay it back.

We shook that place and walked around town, checked out some guys putting a pig in an imu at Kona Inn, then watched the tourists stores getting ready to nail plywood over their windows after

47

they close. I saw Daddy pass in his car, letting every-body know he was around. I waved but he didn't see me.

I looked back toward the pier. Swabbys were crawling off the launch like white ants.

CHAPTER 7

Around lunchtime we decided to head up to Reggie's place. His parents were at work and we could raid the icebox.

As we walked we heard *varoom! Vmm, vmm. Varooooom-blattattatt!* Booley's car, coming up behind us.

We stopped and waited as Booley pulled alongside us and stopped. "Howzit," he said.

"Hey, Boo," I said.

As always, CC was in the backseat, looking like someone from death row. Eyes vacant, nobody home.

Reggie and Kalani stood behind me. Cowards.

49

Booley said, "Where you punks going?"

I said, "I don't know. Reggie's house, prob'ly. Then mines. We gotta get some money. Oh, yeah, we wanted to ask if you could buy us some beer. We pay you double, like last time."

"Where's the money?"

"We only got two dollars, but I got couple more at my house."

"Then let's go get it. Hop in."

Since I was closest, I had to slip in the back and move over next to CC. Then Reggie got in next to me. Smug-face Kalani sat in front. CC glared at me when my arm accidentally rubbed up against the tattooed band around his bulging biceps. Hoo, suddenly it was sweaty hot in that car.

Booley drove away so slow ants were going faster than us. Outside, tourists turned to see what's in that car. They looked nervous.

Then about a minute later we saw Janet and Monica walking on the road. Booley said, "Watch this," and cruised up behind them real quiet. Then, *varoooooom-blatttt!* The girls jumped and shrieked.

Janet and Monica made angry faces, then came and squeezed their heads in the window. "Someday I'm going to strangle you, stupid Booley," Monica said. "So where you going?"

"Who cares? Get in."

"Love to," Monica said. She not afraid of nothing.

Someday she going get in the wrong car. Monica opened the door.

"CC's in the backseat," Booley said.

"Oh . . . Hi, CC," she said, kind of quiet. So maybe she's afraid of *one* person.

CC shoved me over and Monica squeezed in between me and him. Now it was *her* arm I was rubbing up against. My brain was saying *yeah, yeah, yeah*. Her hair smelled like ginger, like pikake, like paradise. Pretty soon I might faint. She sat right up next to me, leaning on me, almost. Maybe because CC was crowding her, or because she secretly loved me. Yeah, that was it.

CC leaned forward and scowled at me with eyes that said I better keep my hands to myself.

Janet got in the front between Booley and Kalani, and Booley started off at a crawl. But you crazy if you think I cared about going anywheres fast with Monica's sweet arm rubbing on mines. I wanted to reach over and put my arm around her neck, and kiss her ear, her cheek. Never in my life did I ever yet kiss a girl. I wanted Monica to be the first.

Bok! CC's hand slapped my head from behind. Ca-ripes, the guy can read minds or what?

I rubbed my head.

When we got to my house, Booley drove up in the yard and stopped on the grass. Everybody got out, doors thumping.

Moms came out of the shed, her hands all muddy with clay.

"Hey, Moms," I called. "Booley gave us a ride."

"Hi, Booley. Hi, girls," she said, wiping her hands on a rag. "Come up on the porch and sit in the shade. I've got some Cokes, if you like." Moms is nice about that, never squawks about my friends coming over.

"Thank you, Mrs. Chock," Booley said, putting his hand on my shoulder like me and him was best buddies.

CC nudged me from behind. "I can use your bat'room?"

"Yeah, sure. Come inside."

Moms said, "Booley, you come, too, help me carry the Cokes." We followed her in, Moms saying to Booley, "How's that little Sissy doing?"

Booley smiled at Moms. "Oh, she's doing good, Mrs. Chock, real good. She going start first grade, you know."

Moms made a face that said *my, my*, then she looked kind of sad. I know she was thinking about how Sissy got no mommy and daddy. Sure it's sad, but Sissy can take care of herself better than plenty of grown-ups I know. And she got Granma and Booley and Reggie and all us guys and half the town as her best friends.

"Follow me," I said to CC.

He went down to the bathroom and I went into

my room and got two more dollars from my coffee-can bank. Then I went to help Moms and Booley carry the Cokes outside.

Monica and Janet were sitting on the steps looking like beauty queens. Reggie was trying to call Daddy's orange cat, Ehu, out from under the house. Ehu means kind of reddish in color. Scared of everything, that cat. Daddy found her on the street by the police station, ratty and starving and crawling with fleas. He said somebody prob'ly dropped her out of a car. Like Moms, Daddy likes cats too, though he won't say he does. Feeds this one scraps from his plate, which drives Moms crazy. Ehu sleeps on Daddy's lap when he reads the paper.

"Here, kiddy kiddy kiddy," Reggie was calling.

I gave Monica a Coke.

She took it and smiled at me. I nearly fell off the steps. "Thanks, Mokes," she said.

I stumbled away to fan my face.

Kalani saw me dizzy and kissed his fingertips again. *Shuddup!* I mouthed.

CC came out of the house and walked way out by the ocean without saying anything.

"Hey, Mokes," Booley whispered, coming up behind me. "You got that money? Reggie gave me his."

I checked to see that Moms wasn't looking and gave Booley the money. He winked at me.

"Where's that other boy?" I heard Moms say. "Eric, go get him a Coke from the icebox."

"I'll get it," Booley said, putting my money in his pocket. He went inside.

"What's that other boy's name?" Moms asked.

"CC."

"Lonely type, huh?"

"Yeah, you could say that."

"What's CC stand for?"

"Calvin Coolidge. But you better not call him that. He don't like that name."

"He *doesn't* like that name, Eric. *Doesn't*. Your language is terrible!"

Booley came back with the Coke. "Take this to CC, Mokes. It's hot out there."

I frowned and took the bottle.

CC watched me walk up. His look reminded me of Kalani's dog Bozo.

"Uh . . . you want this?" I said.

"More of them coming off the boat now," CC said, taking the Coke from me. He sucked down a long gulp, then pointed the bottle down the coast at the destroyer. "Thanks, brah."

Booley whistled, *Pthweeet!* and waved for CC to come. Booley had his shirt in his hand and was showing off his muscles to Janet and Monica, and Monica was checking him out. *Hey, Monica, check mines*, I thought, hurrying back, taking off my shirt

54

too. *Look, I been working out.* But she only looked at Booley.

Booley and CC and Janet and Monica left in Booley's noise-wagon, fat tires kicking up stones.

When they'd gone, the cat came out.

CHAPTER 8

"**S**trange, how Booley's being so nice to us," Kalani said as we started walking up to Reggie's house, where we'd wanted to go in the first place.

"Why?" I said. "Booley can be nice. Before his moms and dad checked out on him he was a real good guy. He saved my life once, too. Remember, Reggie? When he saved me from ghosts?"

"*Ghaa*," Reggie said. "Shuddup about ghosts."

"Booley's scared of ghosts, just like you, Reggie. And of all people, you should know why. But he said ghosts can be good, too."

"He's nuts, man."

"No, he said ghosts sometimes tell you when you're making the wrong move. Booley said it's like you get this voice inside your head that tells you to watch out, or that there's something you got to respect."

Kalani said, "That's what aumakua are all about."

"I don't want to talk about this," Reggie said.

I said, "Okay, but Booley told me how to get rid of a ghost if you don't like it. Scare it. Make a quick move, or scream. If it disappears, it's a ghost. If it doesn't, then it ain't."

"One question, Mokes," Reggie said. "How can I get rid of you?"

"Okay, okay, but Booley ain't so bad, I tell you. That's all."

"Maybe Booley's being nice because he thinks he might die tonight," Reggie said. "Maybe he wanted to tell us he likes us."

"Jeese," Kalani said, scratching the scar in his eyebrow. "You folks are idiots. All he was doing was giving us a ride."

"A last ride," Reggie said.

I wondered if I should tell Daddy about any of this. Then I thought: *Daddy's boy.*

It would be a good, clean fight, that's all.

If I saw it. If it happened before six o'clock.

No, no. Not *if.* I couldn't miss something like that.

* * *

At Reggie's house Janet and Monica were in Janet's room with the radio blasting. Reggie and Kalani walked right past Janet's open door. But not me.

Monica was standing at the mirror with some kind of pencil, drawing on her face and dancing. Janet was dancing too, and putting on lipstick. The whole place smelled like perfume and powder. Janet had on a white shirt with no sleeves, tied at the waist, and jeans shorts. Look nice, man. And Monica had a short blue shirt where you could see her stomach. *Aieee*, so smooth, so sweet, I like use that stomach for a pillow, holy smokes. And also she had on jeans shorts like Janet, and golden earrings, two on one ear and one on the other.

"Mokes," Kalani called from Reggie's room.

But I couldn't take my eyes off Monica.

Janet said, "Hey, Monica, you got a fan."

Monica peeked at me in the mirror. She smacked a kiss, big smoochy lips. Her face said, *Come on over and let me give you a real one.*

Yaaahh!

Reggie grabbed my arm and dragged me away. "They just playing with you, Mokes."

"But—"

"Trust me, they just fooling around." I let him drag me to the kitchen. "Mokes, you so stuck I can't believe it."

From Janet's room I could hear them laughing

over the radio, which was shaking the whole house. *Thoomp, thoomp, thoomp.*

Kalani opened the icebox.

Monica came and leaned in the doorway, arms crossed and grinning.

Janet pushed past her. "You better not eat up all our food, Reggie," she said. "Mom won't like it."

"You should be the one to worry what Mom won't like," Reggie said. "When she finds out you dressing up to fool around with Navy guys, you going had it."

"Who said we were going to fool around with Navy guys?"

Reggie laughed. "What? You think I'm stupid?"

"Okay, so what, then? We're going on the boat, that's all. Just to visit. And you better keep your mouth shut about it. If you get me in trouble, then Monica will tell CC to beat you up, you hear that?"

"Oooo, I scared," Reggie said.

Janet smirked. "You better be scared, little brother. Let's go, Monica. Stinks in here."

Monica, still waiting by the door, looked amused. She saw me staring at her and blew me another kiss. *Mokes, Mokes, Mokes,* she was saying, breathing the words in her head. *I love you.*

At one o'clock we left Reggie's house, crunching Maui chips and drinking cold 7-Ups.

From up by Reggie's you could see the bay over

the top of the trees. The destroyer was sitting out there, so still it looked fake. Another launch was heading in with more white uniforms on it.

Just above the Catholic church we took a shortcut through the graveyard. It was quiet, hot, and full of weeds and centipedes. Even in daytime Reggie hated that place. He said, "If the dead peoples in here could talk, they would be mad as bees because nobody's taking care of this place."

"You couldn't *pay* me to do that job," I said. "Too spooky."

"Hey, Reggie," Kalani said. "How's about tomorrow night you and me set up a tent and camp out here?"

"Go ahead, make fun if you like. But if you ever came in here after dark, and you heard drums or a flute, then it's all over, man. *Fffit!* You history. But there is one thing you can do to live."

Kalani snickered. But then he said, "Okay, what is it?"

"Maybe I won't tell you, since you won't believe it."

"Your brain is so cracked, Reggie. . . . But what is it, anyway?"

Reggie looked both ways, then whispered, "To save youself, you got to take off all your clothes and lie facedown in the dirt."

Kalani laughed.

"Then the obake might let you live," Reggie went on. "If you lucky, Kalani. Which I don't think you would be. The obake know you now. They heard you laugh at them."

That shut Kalani up.

CHAPTER 9

We broke out onto the road just down from Kalani's place.

The sky was cloudless and the ocean smooth and blue. The launch was now heading back out to the destroyer, a bright white wake punching out from under the hull. Ran real nice over that calm sea.

"I gotta get something from my house," Kalani said.

Reggie wiped his forehead. "Anywhere but that graveyard."

Bozo wagged his tail at Kalani and whined, and Kalani grinned at us. "You folks be nice to my doggy, yeah?"

"I hope his old man ain't home," I whispered.

Just then Eddy came back from the dead and started barking. *Arf. Arf. Arf. Arf. Arf. Arf.* I covered my ears. *Arf. Arf. Arf.* Chinese water torture, dripping on your head. *Arf. Arf. Arf.*

"*Kalani!*" I called.

Couple minutes passed before Kalani slouched out wearing his I-am-the-coolest police-style mirror shades.

"What you got those for?" Reggie asked.

"Stare down Navy guys, what else?"

Reggie shook his head. "Yeah, man, you nasty."

"You like me show you some nasty, Reggie?"

"Come on, you stupits," I said. "Let's go."

By two o'clock there must have been about a couple-three hundred sailors all hanging around on the pier and sitting in bars and shopping. The Navy police were strutting around with their SP armbands and nightsticks. Daddy had one of those sticks in his car, a police baton called The Prosecutor.

Everybody was in a pretty good mood. I saw Sergeant Tiumalu laughing with some Navy guys out in front of the Bucket O' Blood. They must have been happy to be on dry ground.

"Let's go see the launch," I said. "Go for a ride out to the destroyer."

Reggie stuck his hand in his armpit and made a fut sound. "Let's go."

Just then Daddy cruised by again. He saw us and stopped and backed up, his arm hanging out the window.

"How's it going, boys?"

We all nodded, okay.

"Good," Daddy said. "Remember our deal, Mokes."

"Yeah, but wait. Can I stay at Kalani's house tonight?"

Daddy tapped his fingers on the door, looking at me. "Sure, just be there by six and stay there."

"Yeah, okay." I blinked and looked down, but only for a second.

Daddy waved and took off, driving slow, like Booley.

"Hey, Mokes," Kalani said. "No way I'm going home at six o'clock."

"You think I am?"

Kalani flicked his eyebrows. "Now you talking, brah."

"Check it out," Kalani said, nodding toward the Bucket O' Blood. Booley and CC were sitting on the seawall across from it, staring at Navy guys. *All right*, I was thinking. Things were warming up.

We climbed up on the seawall. Kalani took off his T-shirt and stuck it in his back pocket. He looked pretty tough in those mirror shades, and so did muscleman Reggie.

When Booley saw us coming, he grinned, his white teeth gleaming. He was cleaning his fingernails with a pearl-handled pocketknife. "Heyyy, junior punks," he said. "I forgot to tell you. The price of beer just went up. Going cost you more."

"Aw, man," Reggie said. "We ain't got no more."

Booley spread his hands apart, the knife under his thumb. "Well . . . if you no like me buy it. . . ."

"No, no," Kalani said. "We'll get some more money."

Booley started to grin, then stopped.

I looked behind me and saw four sailors coming toward us, talking and looking around as if they never seen a fishing town before. Me and Kalani and Reggie sat down next to Booley and CC and scowled as the swabbys came closer. Now I figured out why Kalani wanted those shades. Hard to stare at somebody like that. Specially when they not even bothering you. And what if they got mad?

The sailors shut up when they saw us. All white guys, a couple years older than Booley and CC. They didn't look worried, but they saw that knife. One of them nodded and said, "Nice knife."

Nobody answered.

I wanted to nod and say, *hey*, because they seemed all right, you know? All snappy clean and white in those uniforms. But me and Kalani and Reggie kept our mouths shut, waiting for Booley. One for all, and all for one.

"Well, well," the same guy said. "Five little tough guys, huh?"

Boom! Booley was off that wall. "You got a problem?" Booley said, one inch from the guy's nose.

The other three swabbys closed in. CC came flying off the wall to stand by Booley. Us guys froze.

The sailor stared at Booley, eye to eye, five seconds, six. Then the guy grinned. "Works every time, don't it, boys?" he said to his buddies, still staring at Booley. "Give a little insult and you find out pretty quick who the hotheads are. Shoulda known it was the one with the Cub Scout knife."

Two SPs came up, and one of them stepped in front of the Navy guy. "You want a ticket back to the ship, mister?"

"No sir," the swabby said, snapping up.

"Move along, then. I see you looking for trouble again you're out of here, you got that?"

"Yessir."

The milk bottles took off.

The SP guys checked us out, then walked away.

CHAPTER 10

After a while we split from Booley and went to Granma's babashop to borrow more money. There was a sailor in the chair getting a haircut. Granma was laughing and yakking away like always.

The Navy guy smiled and nodded at us.

Granma said, "Eh, boys, long time no see."

"Granma," Reggie said. "Mokes can borrow some money too?"

I looked at Reggie. Ca-ripes.

Granma said, "Sure, Mokey. How much you need?"

"Uh . . . couple bucks . . . but only for today.

Tomorrow I pay you back." Stupit Reggie. I going cream him.

"What's up, boys?" the sailor said, like he was prob'ly an okay guy. Most of those guys were just doing time, like we might be doing someday.

But gotta be cool, so none of us said anything. Reggie went to the money drawer and took out two dollars and gave it to me and I stuffed it into my pocket.

Just then, Sissy came in with Jeepers in one hand and two red Popsicles in the other. She took one Popsicle to the sailor and gave him some change.

"Thanks, Sissy," he said. "You keep the change."

He winked at us guys, then to Sissy he said, "My daughter is about your age, Sissy. She's a soccer player. Kicks like a mule. How 'bout you? You play any sports?"

Sissy shook her head.

"Sissy play ukulele," Granma said. "She can sing Mary Had a Lamb."

"No kidding," he said. "Can I hear you play?"

Reggie nudged me with his elbow and nodded to the window. Booley and CC were coming up to the babashop. Ho, man.

When Booley came in, Sissy ran over and hugged his legs. Booley put his hand on her head and glared at the Navy guy. But the swabby was still smiling, like he didn't see the hate in Booley's eyes.

"Sissy brudda," Granma told him.

He nodded at Booley. "You have a sweet little sister, son."

Booley was stone-face.

Granma frowned. She stopped snipping and looked at Booley.

Booley said, "Sissy, go outside and play somewhere, go." Sissy took the kitten and her Popsicle and went out, and all the time Booley never took his eyes off the Navy guy.

Granma pointed a comb at him. "*You* go."

Booley still gave him deadly eye.

Granma came up to Booley and stood in front of his face, waiting.

Finally Booley blinked, then left with CC.

"Ne'mind those boys," Granma said to the sailor. "Sissy brudda no like Nabey, yeah?"

He bunched up his eyebrows, how come?

Granma kind of sigh. "The mama of him and that little girl ran away wit' one Nabey mans."

The guy shook his head, looking like he actually felt bad about it.

"And these boys," Granma said, pointing the scissors at us. "They all like grow up, act strong, like those big ones that just le'pt. But look," she said, now smiling. "Still young yet. Cute, no?"

That stupit milk bottle grinned at us and that made us mad.

So we left.

* * *

Now the town was starting to jump.

Fishing boats were coming back in, fish flags flying to show what fish they had on board—marlin, ahi, mahimahi, ono. Tourists and sailors and locals were all over the pier waiting to see the fish. The sun was low on the horizon, making all the colors inside the bay gold and bright and rich. Over by King Kam Hotel three guys were playing Hawaiian music, and behind them, others were setting up a stage for the outdoor concert. Tonight Olomana was going to play, a good Hawaiian band from Honolulu. What a night it was going to be.

Except for six o'clock. *Tst.*

"What time now?" I asked.

Nobody knew. Kalani said, "Listen for the church bell."

"Let's go down by King Kam," Reggie said. "Watch those guys set up. We can check the clock there too."

We drifted over, trying to look cool. We went into the hotel from the back, slinking behind coconut trees and hibiscus hedges. If the manager saw us, he would surely kick us out. We didn't look like no tourists.

But what we saw when we walked in was worse than the manager.

What we saw was trouble.

What we saw was Monica and Janet.

CHAPTER 11

They were sitting with four sailors at a table just outside the bar. *Hey, Monica,* I wanted to shout. *What are you doing?* I felt kind of sick. Kalani put his hand on my shoulder. "Don't mean nothing, Mokes. They just like show off, that's all. Come on. Forget them."

I felt so shaky I couldn't talk. I never had that feeling before.

Monica saw us and waved like she was saying, *Hey, look at us with these Navy officers—cool, yeah?*

Yeah, well, if she thought those guys were officers she got a surprise coming. Those guys were just privates, or whatever the Navy call the low guys.

Reggie made a fist, took a step toward them, but Kalani grabbed his arm. "Not our business, Reggie. Anyways, as long as they stay here nothing going happen."

Reggie said, "Yeah, well, we going baby-sit, then." Funny how Reggie wanted to protect Janet, even though she never listened to him about anything.

"Fine, fine, brah."

I checked around the corner for a clock. Going on five o'clock. Cripes.

Monica and Janet ignored us. "They going be okay, Reggie," Kalani said. "Still daylight, yeah? No need worry yet."

From outside, we heard Booley's car making a loud, spitting rumble. We ran out of the hotel and followed it down the street. Booley saw us in the mirror and pulled up by the Bucket O' Blood. When we got by his window, almost out of breath, he raised up a six-pack of beer.

Kalani reached in for it. "*Primo?* How come you didn't get Oly, or Bud?"

"What? You think you too good for local beer?" Booley said. "Primo is your roots, brah." He was just trying to cover up for buying us the cheapest beer so he could pocket a little more of our cash. "Maybe I shoulda bought you folks *root* beer." He stuck out his hand and I dug out Granma's two bucks.

Booley grinned and handed Kalani the six-pack, then drove away. Down by the church he turned around and headed back toward the pier.

Kalani took off his shirt and covered the six-pack. "Gotta get this on ice."

Up behind the Bucket O' Blood was a big stainless-steel ice maker and two Dumpsters. Nobody was around, so Reggie found a cardboard whiskey box in the garbage and filled it with ice. Kalani buried the beer in it and we took the box down to the Palace Museum and hid it under some coconut leaves that were stacked up by the side of the building. "Hurry it up," I said. "I gotta call somebody."

"Who?"

"Monica."

Granma shook her head when we walked in again. "What'choo boys like this time?"

The Navy man was gone, but in his place was Sergeant Tiumalu.

"Mokes like use the phone," Reggie said.

"You got girlfren, Mokey?" Granma asked.

Sergeant Tiumalu winked at me. "Somebody I know?"

I ignored both of them and took the phone book and stretched the phone cord around the corner.

I found the number for King Kam Hotel and dialed.

"Uh . . . could you please page a guest?" I said, trying to lower my voice. "Just try paging Monica, in the bar area."

I waited and waited and waited and finally Monica answered.

"Hello?" she said, sounding kind of worried.

"Monica," I whispered. "This is Mokes, lissen—"

"What are you doing calling me?"

"Shuddup and lissen. Booley and CC are in town. They might come inside the hotel. If they see you with those swabbys you going be in big trouble."

"Booley and CC don't own me."

Just then I saw Granma's clock. Five-fifteen.

"Lissen to me, Monica. Booley's looking for trouble. Get away from those guys. I gotta go."

CHAPTER 12

Sergeant Tiumalu was just pushing himself up out of the chair when I came out from behind the wall. Jeese, that guy must be close to two hundred fifty pounds. "Looks good, Granma," he said. He gave her ten bucks, almost double.

Then to us, he said, "What's going on, boys?"

"Nothing," all of us said at the same time.

"Nothing, huh?" He chuckled to himself. "Well, listen up. I don't want to see any of you boys in town tonight. We already got enough to worry about."

"Who, us?" Kalani said. "We don't cause no trouble."

75

"Good. So where you going now?"

"Uh . . . Kalani's house," I said. "I going stay there tonight."

"Come, then. I'll give you boys a ride."

Man, man *man!*

When Sergeant Tiumalu drove us up to Kalani's house, somebody slammed the front door shut. Sergeant kind of chuckled and said, "Guess I'm not welcome around here."

"Don't mean nothing," Kalani said, getting out. "He's like that to everybody." Sergeant Tiumalu shook his head and backed out and headed off to town.

Bozo was going nuts, as usual. Then Eddy started. *Arf arf arf arf arf.* And finally Spike, yapping inside. But Spike stopped when Kalani's old man yelled, "*Haaahhhhh!*" at him.

"I ain't going in there," Kalani said.

I agreed with that. Reggie said, "So let's get out of here."

I jumped when the screen door whapped the side of the house. Mr. Douglas charged out, cranked up on booze. You could tell because he was grinning. He must have just been waiting for Sergeant to get out of there so he could leave. He waved at us and headed down the street.

Kalani watched him. "This is the only time he's

nice. Just after he's had a little and just before he's had too much."

When Kalani said that, I remembered Daddy had too much one time, at somebody's wedding reception. Daddy sat on the beach and drank beer with his friends. Pretty soon he was trying to show off his tai chi moves on top of a picnic table. But he couldn't keep his balance. Hoo, was he *funny*, everybody laughing and clapping. Moms took a picture, and now every time she pulls it out to show somebody, Daddy tells her to rip it up. But she won't. Daddy gets so embarrassed he sweats. But that's a different kind of too much than Kalani's old man had.

"So what we going do now?" Reggie asked.

"We can't go back to town," I said.

"Why? I thought you said—"

"I know, but didn't Sergeant just tell us he didn't want to see us in town tonight?"

"Yeah, but what about Booley? We not going see him fight?"

"Sure we going see him fight," Kalani said. "We just got to wait for dark, then sneak back. Ain't that right, Mokeyboy?"

I wanted to be with Kalani and Reggie and Booley. Stand by my friends. But . . .

"I promised I'd stay out of town after six o'clock. It's almost that now."

Reggie laughed, pointing at me. "I knew it, I knew it. See, I told you. Daddy's boy."

"That's Mokes, Reggie," Kalani said. "Too honest for his own good."

"If you futs don't shut up I going take on you both right now," I said.

"Cool your jets, Mokeyboy. We only joking. But really, what you going do? Me and Reggie going back to town. But you can stay inside my house with Spike. We come back later."

Spike? Sheese. "I guess I'll just go home."

"Hey, we'll go with you. After dark me and him can sneak back. And maybe you change your mind."

"Maybe," I said.

CHAPTER 13

We headed down to my place, walking in the middle of the road. When a car came we just bunched up on one side. Everybody around there drove pretty slow, anyway.

Moms was still working in her shed. I didn't want to bother her, so we hit the kitchen and found some apples and a half-empty bag of Fritos and took them into my room. I sat on the floor and leaned against the wall cramming Fritos into my mouth. Kalani lay down on my bed, one hand behind his head and the other rubbing an apple on his T-shirt to make it shine. Reggie sat at my desk, knee bouncing, checking out the small ship-in-a-bottle that Moms gave me when I was a kid.

"How they got this boat in here?" he said.

"Midgets," Kalani said.

"No kidding . . . midgets. Like your brain, yeah, Kalani? Hey, Mokes, what's these bullets for?"

Bullets? "What bullets?"

"These ones." He held up the box and I rememberd this morning when I was cleaning Uncle Randy's .38. The box was open.

I leaped up and grabbed the T-shirt I'd thrown over the gun.

Gone.

"What?" Reggie said, looking up at me. "What's wrong?"

"What'd you do with the gun?"

"What gun? Wasn't no gun here."

Kalani sat up. "You got a gun, Mokes? Let me see it."

"Come on, Reggie, stop joking. Where is it?"

"Really, Mokes. Never had no gun here."

"But . . ."

I looked in the drawer, then on the shelf, then around my desk and on the floor. Nothing. I ran into Daddy's closet, where I'd gotten the gun. Nothing there, either. Maybe Moms had found it and put it in the kitchen. Not there. Not in the living room, not in the bathroom. Not anywhere. My heart was pounding in my throat.

Kalani and Reggie followed me around, saying, "What'choo doing, Mokes? What's wrong?"

"I had a gun." My breathing went short, like gasping. "I was cleaning it . . . this morning. I put it on my desk when . . ." I had to lean over, try to breathe. My hands started to sweat. "When Reggie came over. Now it's gone."

"Maybe your mom put it away," Reggie said.

"No, she didn't know I had it." I ran back to my desk, picked up the bullets. "I hid it here, with these bullets. I wasn't supposed to take it out."

"Maybe you forgot where you hid it," Reggie said.

"No, it was on the desk, I tell you."

Ask Moms, I thought. Yeah. Maybe she *did* find it. "Wait," I said. "I'll be right back." I ran out to the shed.

Moms was sitting on a stool by her kiln. She looked up when I came in. I tried to calm down. "Hi, Eric," she said, then checked her watch. "Right on time."

"M-Moms, did you see a . . . Did you find Uncle Randy's gun in my room and take it somewhere?"

"His gun? You're not supposed to take it out, Eric. You know that."

"Yeah, but—but how's about Daddy? Did he come home today? And go in my room?"

"He hasn't been home all day. What's this all about?"

"Uh . . . well . . . nothing. I was just cleaning it this morning, and now I can't find it. It's prob'ly in my room somewhere. I'll go look again."

Moms wiped a bead of sweat from her hairline with the back of her hand. "Give me another hour and I'll come make some dinner. And you find that gun *now*, and put it away, safe, Eric. You hear me?"

I nodded and ran back to my room. An ugly thought started to grow in my head. Maybe . . . maybe . . .

Reggie and Kalani looked up.

"I think I got a big problem," I said.

Reggie said, "You mean, besides your face?"

I paced back and forth in my room. "Remember today when Booley came over? And remember he came in to get that Coke for CC? Well, what if . . . What if he came in my room? . . . And what if he took that gun? It was right here with those bullets, I tell you."

Yeah, now that I thought about it. It had to be Booley. What if he wanted more than a fight? What if . . . *Jeese!*

"Maybe he wants to shoot somebody," Reggie said.

"No, no, no. Booley's not like . . . Is he?" I started sweating all over. *Please*, let me be wrong. I *had* to be wrong. "We gotta find Booley," I said. I started for the door. "If he took it and my old man finds out, I going had it bad, man. Real bad. And Booley too."

"Wait, wait, wait," Kalani said. "We can't go now. Too light. We gotta wait till dark so we can hide, remember? From Sergeant . . . and your daddy, Mokes."

My hands were trembling now.

Reggie said, "Calm down, man. We'll find the gun."

We waited for dark.

Pacing, sweating, sitting, rocking back and forth with my arms folded into my stomach. Waiting was the hardest thing I ever had to do in my life. Thinking about Uncle Randy's .38 gave me stomach cramps. If Booley did have it, he was on the road to taking me down, and himself—*way* down. Like I said, I know a couple things about Booley.

One of them is, I know that Leonard Biao is missing half a finger because Booley shot it off. Booley keeps quiet about it, and Leonard sure ain't going tell nobody. Make him look like a stupit. I only know about it because Daddy told me. But the war between those two guys has become a legend, almost.

They used to be friends. Actually, they were cousins. But one day about three years ago Leonard wanted to go play pool up in Kainaliu. Booley didn't want to go, but Leonard talked him into it. That pool hall was also a bar, so Leonard and Booley couldn't get in, which was just fine with Booley. But, ho, Leonard got all psycho over it and went back for revenge.

Late that night, dragging Booley with him, he broke into the pool hall and cut up the tables with a broken beer bottle. Booley didn't do that part, just Leonard. But ca-ripes, Leonard got no brains, not only because he cut up the tables, but also because everybody in the pool hall that day saw those two guys get kicked out and knew they had bad blood about it. So guess where the police went first.

But here's where the *real* bad blood came. Sergeant Tiumalu went to Leonard's house to question him about it, and Leonard said, yeah, he was there, but it was *Booley* who cut the place up, not him.

So Sergeant went to see Booley, and *man*, did Booley lose it. Sergeant had to take him in handcuffed. Booley ended up with one-year probation and a thousand-dollar fine. Leonard just got probation. Six months.

A couple weeks after he got arrested, Booley went up to Leonard's place and he and Leonard got into a monster fight. Leonard's moms called the police, and this time it was Daddy who went. Leonard had a pellet gun and pulled it on Booley, and Booley grabbed Leonard's arm and tried to take it away. This was before Daddy got there. Well, Booley got the gun away from Leonard, all right, but while he was doing it, the gun went off and shot off half of Leonard's left-hand first finger.

Daddy found Leonard rolling around on the ground, blood all over his hands and Booley standing over him with the gun. Daddy took the gun away, then drove Leonard to the hospital. He had to lock Booley in his car, because Booley refused to say a word about anything and looked like he still wanted to kill Leonard.

Leonard said it was an accident. So Daddy gave Booley a break, telling him he would be the sorriest boy on this island if he ever caught him with a gun again. And not only that, Daddy said Booley had to come talk to him at our house once a month for a year, in *addition* to his probation for the pool hall.

Funny thing is, Booley came. Always on time. They sat out by the ocean so they could talk in private. I never heard what they said. Except once.

CHAPTER 14

The road back to town was so dark you could hardly see it. When cars came we stumbled into the ditch to hide, even Reggie, who didn't want to go near the night noises in the bushes. Me, I didn't care because I felt sick about lying to Moms about going to Kalani's, like I lied to Daddy.

"Obake!" Kalani shouted suddenly, scaring me and Reggie spitless. He thought that was so funny.

"You stupit Kalani," Reggie said. "Now you *called* them. Now they going come."

"You know, Reggie," Kalani said, wiping the tears from his eyes, "you need to see a shrink, man."

"How many times I got to tell you, you dingdong?

You can't joke around like that. Now you disturbed them and now we got to protect ourselves."

"Come on, Reggie," I said. "Stop trying to scare us. We got more important things to worry about."

"This is what we got to do: Spit and swear and stay in the middle of the road. Then the ghosts will leave us alone."

"You are *so* nuts, man," Kalani said.

"Okay, *you* walk by the bushes, then. Don't do nothing." Reggie went out to the middle of the road and started spitting and swearing. *Ptoooth.* "Fut." *Ptoooth.* "Butthead."

I followed him to the middle of the road. *Ptooth.* "Shucks."

"Shucks?" Reggie said. "That's a swear?"

"Okay." *Ptoooth.* "Kukae."

"That's better."

Kalani shook his head. But he might change his mind if we saw some obake. So by spitting and swearing and walking in the middle of the road we made it to town.

Kalani put his hand out to stop us. "Look. Monica."

We stepped into the shadows on the side of the road. It was Monica, all right, walking into the glow of a light just down the street. Janet was right behind her.

And with them, two milk bottles.

Monica glanced around to see if anyone was looking, then grabbed one guy's hand and pulled him quickly across the street to the dark grounds of the old missionary church. Janet and the other swabby followed them.

We checked if anyone was coming, then came out of the shadows and headed down to the church, which was separated from the street by a rock wall and a grassy yard. We ran to hide, squatting down behind the wall and looking across the grass to the stone-sided church. Dim yellow lights glowed in the windows.

"Cop coming," Kalani said, peeking around the wall. "Your old man."

The radio spit out a crackly voice as his car sped by.

We crept up to the empty church and filed in slowly, looking down the pews. No Monica, no Janet. We went out back.

"Maybe they went through to the back street," Reggie said.

"Shhh," Kalani said, putting his finger to his lips. Back out on the street you could hear a car rumbling slowly by.

"Booley," Reggie whispered.

Then we spotted dark shadows on a bench.

Reggie squinted. "Is that you, Janet?"

"What are you, my mother?"

"Who are those guys?"

"None of your business. Get out of here."

Kalani grabbed Reggie's arm and started pulling him away. "Let's go, Reggie. You can't live her life for her."

Reggie yanked his arm out of Kalani's grip, but followed us anyway, walking backwards, staring at the four shadows.

Back out on the street, Sergeant Tiumalu and Rocky Machado both raced by in their cars, going the same way as Daddy. "Something going on," Kalani said.

With all the police gone we got brave and walked out on the street.

Some of the stores had big sheets of plywood up over the windows. But the tourist traps were still open and crowded. The Bucket O' Blood was crazy with guys bunched up outside on the street. It was so packed Kalani's cousin Robert had to stand at the door to keep people from coming in.

When Robert saw us he waved. "Can you believe this place?" he yelled over the blast of old-time rock and roll.

Kalani shouted, "You seen Booley?"

"Down the pier, I think."

"What's with the cops?"

"Car crash." Robert beefed his way in front of a drunk-as-a-skunk swabby trying to get inside. "Not yet, brah," Robert told the guy. "Somebody gotta come out before somebody can go in. Fire code."

The sailor tried to shoulder through anyway, but Robert pushed him back and he staggered into some other sailors, who laughed and shoved him back at Robert. Robert shook his head and put his arm on the guy's shoulder. He said something and they both laughed. Robert should be a cop. So smooth with drunks.

Reggie spotted Booley's car on the pier.

I woke up: *Get the gun!* I had to pay attention. Booley, why'd you take the gun, man? *Why?*

I kept flashing back to this memory of one time when Booley came for his monthly talk with Daddy after he shot off Leonard Biao's finger. That day it started to rain, and Daddy and Booley came in and talked in the front room. I went into the kitchen to listen, pretending to be looking for something to eat. Moms caught me and kicked me out, but not before I heard one part.

"No," Booley was telling Daddy. "He didn't try to run."

Who, I wondered? Funny, the way they talked, long silences after Daddy said something. Maybe Booley was thinking of exactly what he wanted to say.

Daddy said, "What'd he do? Fight?"

Silence.

Then, "He face him down. The guy backed off."

"And CC had a gun?"

"Only a small .22, look like a German Luger."

"But he didn't pull it to make the guy leave?"

"No."

Now Daddy was silent.

Finally, he said, "You have a gun, Booley?"

"No, I don't have no gun, but if I did I would give it to you. For real, Chief. I told you way back I would never fool around with them, and I meant what I said. I meant it."

"Okay, Booley. Believe it or not, son, I'm proud of you. For six months now you've been coming over here to talk. You come on time and you don't lie to me. Your father would be proud of you too."

There was a long silence after that.

Then Daddy said, "Why do you hang around with CC, Booley?"

"Nobody likes him. I feel sorry for him. We go way back, you know, me and him."

There was a pause, then Booley added, "I don't know, Chief. I guess I just hate to see him go down. You know what I mean?"

Now Daddy was quiet.

I imagined him sitting there staring at the floor.

Almost whispering, Daddy said, "Yeah. I know what you mean, son."

Now me, Reggie, and Kalani headed over toward the pier, looking, looking. Where's Booley? We climbed up on the seawall and walked along the top.

Under my feet the salt-scratchy concrete was still warm from the sun. On one side of that wall the ocean was sleeping, with dark sky above and pin-prick stars poking through. But on the other side, the town was dancing and shoving and swearing. Down by the pier you could hear sweet Olomana playing at King Kam. And somewhere out there Booley was walking around looking for trouble, and I prayed it wasn't with Uncle Randy's .38.

Only one light was on at the pier, and it was way down at the end. From where we stood in the dark part you could see Olomana in the lights of their outdoor stage. Flowers, drums, speakers, spotlight reflections flashing off guitars. Big crowd, mostly local people, but with lots of white uniforms speckled in it.

We walked up to Booley's car. Real casual.

It was dark inside, couldn't see anybody. "Hey, Boo," I called. "You in there?"

No answer.

I crept closer and peeked in the chopped window.

"Maybe they went to hear Olomana," Reggie said.

I glanced around the pier. Then, quickly, I opened the door and stuck my hand under the front seat. Only a crowbar. No gun. Kalani went around to the other side and checked under the seat there. He shook his head.

92

"Try the glove compartment," I said. "Hurry."

Nothing there, either. I slapped my hand on the roof.

"Hey, look!" Kalani said.

There was a fight down at the Bucket O' Blood.

CHAPTER 15

By the time we ran over there the SPs had already broken it up. Just Navy guys. Where was Booley? Now I was getting scared.

"Hey," Kalani said, making drinking motions with his hand.

"Forget that," I said. "We got to find Booley."

"Only take a minute, Mokes. Lighten up, man."

So we went back down along the seawall to the Palace and dug out our sagging cardboard-box cooler from under the coconut leaves. The ice was melted, but the beer was cold. Six sweating bottles.

"One for you, one for you, and one for me," Kalani said.

Never yet in my life did I down more than half of one beer. Daddy didn't say I couldn't do it. He said, "Look around the bars, Eric, and see what that stuff can do to you." I saw what he meant. But that wasn't going to be me. No way.

I twisted off the cap and took a swig. *"Aaachh!"* Nasty. "Stuff bites, man."

"Yeah, good, yeah?" Kalani said, pumping his eyebrows.

"Here, Mokes," Reggie said. "If you don't like that, try this." From his shorts pocket he pulled out that rolled-up paka Leonard Biao gave us.

"Jeese, Reggie," Kalani said. "I thought you got rid of that."

"I wanted to try it."

"Hide it!" I said. "You want to get us *arrested*?"

Reggie pulled out some matches and lit it and sucked in some smoke. He held it in and handed the paka to Kalani, who looked at it a second, then shrugged and sucked some smoke in and gave it to me. "How come you know how to do it?" I asked Reggie.

"Janet," he squeaked, letting the smoke out.

I looked at it, small and light as a dead scorpion. Daddy would kill me with his bare hands if he saw me with this. He'd squeeze my neck so hard my eyes would pop out. But I took it and sucked on it and held the smoke in like Reggie and Kalani did. Say Daddy's Boy to *that*, I thought. I let out the smoke. I didn't feel any different. "Junk," I said, and gave it back to Reggie.

"Give it some time."

We all did it a couple times again. Pretty soon I was starting to feel a little bit funny. Kind of tingly. Hoo.

When the paka was gone, Reggie twisted open his beer and took a long gulp. He turned and looked at the bar. Loud music, loud voices, shoving. "Those guys been on that boat so long they cross-eyed. They going get plastered like you, yeah, Mokes?"

"What?"

I was really starting to feel kind of out there. You know, happy and dizzy, almost like I was floating. Kalani and Reggie were looking so nice and friendly I wanted to hug them.

Reggie patted my head. "S'okay, Mokes. Go back to sleep."

Kalani put his arm around my shoulder. "Come, we go back down King Kam, find Booley."

"Huh?"

"Shee, don't take nothing to give you a buzz, yeah, Mokeyboy?"

Kalani stuck an extra beer in my back pocket. "Hide the open one in your hand," he said. "Keep it close to your side."

Everybody over at the Bucket was having a good time, lights and music and shouting in the sweet-smelling nighttime air. *Yeah!* I was thinking. *Let's go!*

Just as we jumped up on the seawall, I looked behind me and saw Monica and Janet walking out from the churchyard with those two sailors hanging all over them. I started to wave at them, feeling friendly now, but Kalani pulled my arm.

Just down the seawall, across from the Bucket O' Blood, was Booley and CC. "Heyyy," I said, as if they could hear me.

Kalani laughed and said to Reggie, "Already he forgot about that gun."

"Gun?" I said.

"You having fun?" Reggie asked, patting my back, and I said, "A-straight, I am," or something stupit like that.

We stumbled down toward Booley and CC, me feeling brave, and cool as Booley, slouching along the seawall like I was tough, like I owned the place.

" 'Ey, Boo," Kalani said. "Howzit?"

We sat down next to him and CC. I tried to work up some stink eye of my own for the sailors across the street. But it was hard. I just wanted to smile. The Navy guys ignored us, anyway, except for the two SP guys leaning against the stone wall with their arms crossed. Kalani set his beer down with a clink and put on his police mirrors . . . police . . . police. Wasn't there something about police? No . . . a police gun?

Just then, on the same side of the street as us, six sailors were coming our way. Dressed white and clean. When they came by us one of them looked up and nodded, *howzit*.

"What'choo looking?" Booley said, spitting the words. I'm going, *Ho, here it comes*.

The haole guy said, "What?"

Booley jumped down off the wall and put his face in front of the guy. "I said, what'choo looking? You got a problem with your ears, milk bottle?"

Now the guy looked mad. "You want me to have a problem, boy?"

"Fricken smart mout', you," Booley said. He shoved the guy back.

The guy balled up his fists. His eyes went cold. His five buddies stepped up beside him, and CC came off the wall like lightning. Then me. Then Kalani and Reggie. Gotta stand by your friends.

Somebody grabbed my shoulder and shoved me out of the way. An SP with his nightstick out. Man, those guys were quick. "Move along," he told the swabbys. "Let's go."

They left with stink looks that said, *We going get you punks later. Oh yeah.*

The SP burned hard into Booley's eyes. "The next time I see you trying to pick a fight, you're going to be meeting up with your local police. How old are you, anyway?"

When Booley didn't answer, the SP tapped his baton on Booley's chest, then walked back across the street toward the Bucket O' Blood.

I took a gulp of beer and noticed my hand was shaking. The paka and beer were wearing off. I took another gulp. "Hey, Boo, we scared him good, yeah?" I said.

Booley looked at me, then took my beer and chugged down half and gave it back. Then he grabbed my T-shirt in his fist. "What'choo know about anything?"

"I . . . I . . ."

"Shuddup!"

Booley let go, and I staggered back. Kalani shook his head.

I left with Kalani and Reggie and went out on the pier, thinking, What did I do? What am I doing here, anyway?

We sat around in the dark, me looking over at the blurry outdoor concert going on at King Kam. Olomana was still going strong, and the crowd was swelling. And on the pier, lovers were spread out in private places, glued together in the shadows and parked cars. The small bay between us and the hotel was glassy, and the torches staked around the beach shot reflecting spears out to us, wobbling on the dark water. I wiped my hand over my face. Maybe it was me that was wobbling.

Reggie said, "When Pops finds out about Janet, he going beat her."

I took another swig of beer.

"Dangerous for her to hang around those guys," Kalani said. "What if they try something?"

Reggie snickered. "She ain't no angel. She can take care of herself."

Kalani and Reggie finished up their first beers and flipped the bottles in the water. I chugged mines and pulled out number two. I was feeling pretty good. Brave enough to rescue Monica. *Help, Mokes, help me*, she would cry, hanging on me for protection. *Save me.*

I took another drink. That Primo was tasting better now. Drinking my roots.

"Mokes, you better slow down," Reggie said.

"Why?"

"Well, one reason is you jumped down with Booley, ready to fight. I wasn't going jump down, you know. But you went so I went. I thought you wanted to be a cop, not a troublemaker."

"Hey, those guys were causing trouble, man."

"How? What they was doing?"

I couldn't remember. "Okay, not them, but those other guys. Messing with Monica."

Kalani took my beer from me and held it out over the edge of the pier and let it gurgle into the sea. "I think you had enough, punk."

"Hey," I said. "That's mines."

A man stumbled out of the shadows on the pier. Kalani turned to see what I was looking at.

"Ca-ripes," he whispered.

CHAPTER 16

Quickly, Kalani slipped over the side of the pier and hung out of sight on a truck-tire boat bumper.

The man came closer.

Mr. Douglas, Kalani's old man. Red-eye drunk. He staggered up and poked Reggie in the chest with a stick. "You theen my boy?"

Reggie knocked the stick away and Mr. Douglas grinned at him. Then he took a long haul on a bottle. He spit in the water and said, "Backit th' bar th' tole me th' theen 'im wif you punkth."

"Like we'd tell you if we knew," I mumbled.

"You th' cop'th kid, yeah?"

Kalani's old man checked me out so long I had to turn away.

"An' rinkin' beer," he said. "Wha' would jer daddy thay?"

I spread my hands apart. "I don't have no beer."

Mr. Douglas snickered.

Then, quick as an eel, he lunged over and slapped the stick down on the truck tire, *whop! whop! whop!* Kalani yelped as it stung his hands. Then, *splash!* he fell in.

Reggie and I jumped up and ran to the edge of the pier.

"Come'n up out of there," Mr. Douglas said.

Reggie reached down to give Kalani a hand, but Mr. Douglas yanked him back. Reggie brought his fists up, but stopped.

Kalani dragged himself up over the edge, dripping, his left hand cut and bloody. He stood tall, facing his old man.

Mr. Douglas glared back. "Don' gif me tha' eye. Git 'ome!" He whacked Kalani's neck.

I winced. *Ow!*

Kalani swung.

Whop! One good slug and Mr. Douglas went down. And out.

We stood gaping. First time in my life I ever saw a kid deck his pops. "He going kill you when he wakes up," Reggie said.

Kalani said, "Gimme me a hand," and together

we dragged Mr. Douglas to a boat trailer and leaned him up against one of its tires.

"Let him sleep it off. When he wakes up he won't even remember how to take a leak." Kalani looked at his father a second, then shook his head. "Loser."

"I was close to popping him myself," Reggie said.

I squinted across the water. Made me dizzy to look that far, everything kind of fuzzy. "Is that Janet and Monica?" It looked like them.

"Yeah . . . and check who's over there."

From the opposite direction, Booley and CC came strolling out of the ABC store and headed toward the Bucket O' Blood.

"Ai-yah," Reggie said. "If Booley sees them with those sailors . . ."

"All right!" I said. "About time Booley going fight."

"Mokes," Kalani said. "That's the beer talking. You forgot about that gun?"

"Come," Reggie said, taking my arm. He led me over to a spigot on the pier and turned it on. Water shot out onto the harbor. "Stick your head in that."

"But . . ."

"Shuddup and do it."

I stuck my head in the water. It blasted out and slapped my face. *Wake up, wake up.* I stood back, shook my head, my T-shirt soaked around the neck.

Reggie turned off the water. "Feel better now?"

I was getting a headache.

"Just follow us, Mokeyboy," Kalani said, starting toward the ABC store and its bright lights.

"Uh-oh," Reggie said. "Look."

Two cars creeping toward us, cruising the street. Leonard Biao. And his mountain boys.

"That's all we need," Kalani said.

Booley and CC, who were almost down at the Bucket O' Blood now, stopped and stared when the two cars went past and out to the pier.

We jumped up on the seawall and went down to where Booley and CC were sitting drinking beer across from the Bucket O' Blood.

"Hey," Kalani said, shaking Booley's hand macho-man style. Booley was back to himself again. Not mad, but smiling.

"Boo," I said. "I . . ."

Booley turned toward me, waited.

"Uh . . . I'm sorry for . . ."

Booley's eyes went soft, like maybe he felt bad about grabbing my shirt. I breathed a little easier. "Forget it," he said. "Those swabbys just got me going. Here, sit, you punks."

We sat and it started coming back to me, about the gun . . . the gun, the gun. . . . Oh, man. *Ask him, ask.*

"Boo," I said. "Today, at my house . . . on my desk there was—"

"Hey, Mokes," CC said.

Everybody looked at him, surprised. CC hardly ever spoke, even to Booley.

CC grinned.

Slowly, his eyes still glued to mine, he raised his T-shirt off Uncle Randy's .38, stuck in his shorts.

CHAPTER 17

Police-blue steel. Checkered hand grip, snake inlay.

"I gave it a name," CC said. "Enforcer. You like that?" He covered it up, checking around to see if anyone had seen.

I prob'ly looked like I was about to shi-shi my pants. If my mind was ever fuzzy, it wasn't anymore.

CC grinned. "You should learn how to hide things better," he said.

"Where you got that gun, CC?" Booley said.

"Mokes's house."

"You stole it? From the *chief's* house? Are you crazy?"

CC looked hurt. "Hey, I just borrowed it for shaking up milk bottles."

Booley stared at him. Maybe he was thinking if it was a good idea to scare swabbys with the gun, or maybe he was remembering Leonard Biao's finger, or his promise to Daddy. I don't know.

Just then Sergeant Tiumalu's car came cruising down the street. I hid behind Kalani, who hid behind Booley. I peeked out as Sergeant drove past. He looked up at Booley and nodded. No smile. He smells trouble.

After Sergeant went by, Booley chugged down the rest of his beer and said, "We looking for Janet and Monica. You folks saw them anywhere?"

Reggie pointed toward the church. "Over there. In the back."

Booley eased himself up.

Gun gun gun gun gun boomed like a cannon in my head.

We headed over toward the church, Booley and CC leading the way. A mongoose ran across the road and slipped into a crack in the rock wall as we went inside the church.

Booley checked around the back and CC walked the aisles, looking down the rows. Maybe he thought Janet and Monica would be lying inside there with the swabbys. Janet and Monica weren't *that* crazy.

107

CC shook his head that no one was up front, so Booley went out back, us guys following. It was quiet and dark. Starry sky, shadowy bushes. But no shadows where we'd seen Janet and Monica before.

CC came running out. "I seen 'um! I seen 'um!"

All of us ran back through the church and out the other side to the street. Janet was just going into the alley to Granma's place. The swabby was with her. No Monica. CC took off, and we ran after him.

Two SPs saw us coming and got ready, slapping their sticks in their hands. But we turned up the alley before we got to them.

We found two sailors in the alley, but not the ones who were with Janet and Monica. One was so drunk he was barfing. His friend was standing next to him, waiting. His eyes jumped around when we surrounded him. CC slammed him against somebody's back door, his fists nearly ripping the guy's white shirt off. "You seen two guys with two girls?"

The sailor, now looking like he might be sick too, pointed up toward the babashop. CC let him go.

The babashop was locked. CC banged on the door with his fist. *Bam! Bam! Bam! Bam! Bam!*

"Wait!" Reggie said.

CC looked at Reggie like, You better get this door open or I going break it down, so Reggie called, "Granma! It's me, Reggie. Open the door."

He knocked loudly. "Granma, open up."

CC shoved Reggie away and slammed the door

with his shoulder. I got a glimpse of the gun when he hit it.

"Hey, what'choo doing?" somebody yelled.

We whipped around. Granma and Sissy, carrying the kitten, hurried up to us. "Reggie, what'choo boys doing?"

"We looking for Janet. We thought she went inside the babashop."

"What you got Sissy out here for, old lady?" Booley said, scowling at Granma. "You no can see the Navy in town?"

Granma checked Booley, scowling back. "If you looking for trouble, I can find it for you. I going call the police."

Booley mashed his lips together and squatted down to Sissy. "What you doing out here, Sissy? You know when the boats come to town you supposed to stay inside. Could be trouble from all these guys drinking."

Sissy's eyes were big as plates.

Booley looked at her a long time, then scratched the kitten's head. "Where you got that?" he asked.

"Mokes gave it to me. Her name is Jeepers."

Booley studied Sissy a moment, then hugged her and stood up. "Sorry, Granma," he said. Then to CC he said, "We go."

We all went back down to the street by the Bucket O' Blood, then crossed over to the seawall. Booley's six-pack of beer was still there. He took one out and pried off the cap with his teeth, spit it out.

The SPs saw us and came strutting down the street.

Then I saw them, Janet and Monica and their lover boys—*inside* the Bucket O' Blood. *Jeese!* How did Robert miss that? They must have gone in the back. Yeah, when they went up the alley.

I *prayed* that CC didn't see them. Because of what was under his shirt.

But Monica saw *us*, her mouth open, like she was saying *oh*. Still now I see that mouth, round and shocked as a dead fish eye.

CHAPTER 18

Too late. CC came off that wall like a lightning bolt.

"What!" Booley shouted, jumping down. His beer bottle rolled off the wall and broke on the concrete below.

The SPs looked up when they heard the breaking glass. CC ran into the street, then Booley. The SPs pushed to meet them, shoving sailors out of the way. Fifteen or twenty milk bottles clumped up to join the SPs. They must have been watching us too.

Reggie jumped down. Then Kalani, and me, thinking, *I got to get that* gun!

Now Booley saw Monica and Janet, trying to get

their two guys to go out the back. But those swabbys weren't going anywhere.

Booley and CC faced up to the SPs with their sticks and their armbands and their rat-eyes jumping around. "Far as you go, boys," one of the SPs said.

Booley checked them out, looking like he was wondering which one he going take down first. Monica, Janet, and their two sailors were coming outside now, followed by half the guys in the bar.

Everybody started bunching around to see. When Monica's swabby came out, CC yelled, "I going get'choo! I going get'choo!" All red in the face. All I could think was *gun gun gun*, my heart pounding right out of my chest.

The swabby yelled back to CC, "Anytime, monkey, here I am!" He hugged Monica closer. Monica was trying to push away and get out of there. Janet was leaving too. "Hey, where you going?" her guy called, but she ran toward the alley, then up by the babashop.

"Let me go!" Monica said, pushing; but the swabby pulled her out to the street, saying, "Don't let these chimps scare you, honey," plenty loud. One of the SPs blocked him with his stick.

CC started to pull that gun, but Booley yelled, "*No!*" grabbing CC's arm. CC backed down. I was sweating like a pig. My hands, my legs, shaking, trembling.

The other SP stepped up and tried to stop Booley

and CC from coming closer, and CC lost it, charging and swinging at the SP's face. *Pow! Pow! Pow!* Cracked him on the ear, the nose. *Bok! Bok!* The SP fell on the sidewalk. CC jumped on him and they rolled out into the street. *Whop!* The other SP came down on CC's head with his nightstick. CC yelped and fell away, grabbing his shaved head in his hands, getting up on his knees, then stumbling back down. Blood started coming through his fingers, streaking down his face.

Booley grabbed the SP, took his stick, and started swinging it at him and at the crowd of swabbys who were trying to jump in the action.

"Let me *go*!" Monica yelled. *"Booley!"*

The swabby was dragging Monica out to the street now, the crowd opening up to let them pass. "You want her?" the guy said to Booley. "Come get her."

Booley threw the nightstick away and charged the guy.

The SP tried to break it up. A sailor picked up the stick and whacked Booley's back with it, right by the kidneys. Booley yelped and went down, grabbing his back. The sailor was just about to hit him again when Robert grabbed the guy's hand, saying, "Hit him again and your head's coming off."

The sailor jerked away, but he didn't hit Booley again.

Kalani helped Booley up, Booley blinking and wobbling. Reggie went to help CC. We limped away with them, up toward the babashop, me sweating with relief.

And I thought: *Gun!*

I reached under CC's shirt and pulled it out and ran.

CC threw Reggie aside and leaped after me, grabbing a fistful of my hair. He dragged me to the ground. I tried to scramble up, the gun in one hand, falling backwards. With blood dripping down his face, CC put one hand around my neck and squeezed. "You going die right now if you don't give that back."

"No," I squeaked.

Bok! CC slapped the side of my head and grabbed the gun out of my hand. I saw him grinning through the little white stars popping in my eyes. CC put the gun back under his shirt and stood over me.

"You okay, Mokes?" Reggie said, helping me up.

"No."

Booley knocked on Granma's door.

We saw Janet hiding in that dark doorway where the sick sailor had spilled his stomach. The smell was all over the place. She ran out when she saw it was us. "Monica," she said, sobbing. "She was drinking. . . . Those guys . . ."

"Aiyee!" Granma said when she opened the door and saw CC all bloody. "I tole you, I tole you. Nabey mans trouble, I tole you."

Booley tried to stand up straight, but couldn't. He

stumbled into the babashop and went over to the chair and knelt down with his head on the seat, hands on his kidneys. CC went to look in the mirror, his shirt stained with blood. The side of my head felt hot and numb, and my ear was ringing.

"I going kill that guy," Booley said.

"Hush," Granma said. "No talk like that. You sit. I call police."

"No, Granma," Booley said.

"But they hurt you, they—"

"We going take care of this ourself."

CHAPTER 19

We left the babashop in a pack and followed Booley down past Kona Inn, down to a dark parking lot with lots of coconut trees. Booley needed to let the pain work out of his back and think of how he could go back and catch Monica's sailor.

So we hung around there ten, twenty minutes, in the dark. Booley and CC sat off from us, talking low, planning. Booley said, loud, "I don't want to *touch* that gun. Give it back to Mokes. Stupit you took it."

I stood up and edged over to them. *Yeah*, I thought. Give it to me. Give—

Just then Leonard Biao's cars crept into the parking lot.

One had those same cut-down windows like Booley's. It was packed with guys. And so was the other car.

Inside all I could see was deadly eyes stabbing back out at me. The sweet stink of crazy weed came from those shadows. Nobody saying howzit, nobody giving shaka sign.

Both cars opened up. Eleven dark guys got out, one after the other. Dark hair, dark shirts, dark pants, dark eyes, dark faces. They checked me out with long stares: *Shark Bait*.

"We saw you eat it," Leonard said to Booley. "Those sailorboys too much for you?" A low rumble of snickers ran through his snakes.

Booley gave Leonard a deadly look.

Leonard didn't even blink.

Out on the dark ocean I could see the lights from the destroyer stretching across the water to shore, bright and clear. So peaceful out there. And my stomach was crawling.

Leonard waited, his grim smile pushing Booley.

"I going take one guy down," Booley finally said. "That's my business. Stay out of my way. If you guys like fight too, that's your business. But what I do ain't no concern of yours."

Leonard nodded silently, looking at the ground and sucking his teeth. Then he looked up and said, "You no mind us watch, yeah?"

Booley said, "Just stay out of my way."

Leonard grinned.

Booley and CC started down the street toward the Bucket O' Blood, us with them, and eleven snakes behind us. Ho, man, if Daddy saw me with that bunch I would be had-it for sure. *Had! It!*

We passed by the row of shops bright and crowded with tourists and sailors who had no idea what's about to go down.

Get the gun, get the gun, get the gun, I kept thinking.

Eleven jungle assassins and five of us must have made a powerful sight. You could see it in the scared faces watching us go by. Even the sailors were looking worried. I was all confused, thinking, *Get the gun;* then, *Man, this is so cool;* then, *What if Daddy comes?;* then, *Pow! Booley going take 'um down;* and then, *Gun!*

We jumped up on the seawall and walked down toward the Bucket O' Blood. Booley stopped to check things out. Small waves made easy thumping sounds against the rocks below, thumping and sloshing. For all the bad stuff going on, it was real nice. Stars and lights from a couple boats winked out on the horizon, way out past the destroyer. Except for how I felt about Monica, all my stony-high braveness was gone and I wanted to be out there too, fishing or sleeping or playing cards. Anything.

Now Monica and the Navy guy were in the crowd outside on the sidewalk. Robert was watching them from the door. From what I could tell it didn't look like Monica was worried about anything anymore. Janet was back too, with the same sailor, only now she was ignoring him, trying to talk to Monica.

My mouth almost dropped off my face when I saw Monica kiss her swabby, right out in the open. *No, no, no, Monica, stop!*

CC saw too. A bulging vein shot down his forehead to between his eyes.

When the Navy guy gave Monica a drink from his glass I knew why she was kissing him. Five other swabbys laughed when Monica took that drink, all of them looking at her like they counting the minutes to when they could get their hands on her too. I could feel CC ready to explode. I wished Leonard was *with* us, that him and his killers were our best friends, our brothers. I wanted eels, sharks, barracudas. I wanted manglers, stranglers, and executioners.

Nobody moved.

Then Booley and CC stepped out on the sidewalk.

The rest of us waited on the seawall above them, lined up shoulder to shoulder. *Now* the Navy guys didn't ignore us. *Now* they were looking. I can't even start to tell how that felt. Inside I was nervous and scared. But also I felt like a bull, specially since I didn't see those SPs anywheres. I even for a moment forgot about the gun.

I spotted Rocky's police car back in town, now out on the pier, lights flashing. Something going on out there. Sergeant's car pulled up behind him. Forget them. They don't see us.

Monica's swabby called, "Monkeys!" and raised his glass to us. "You came back. Anybody got a banana?"

Now there were fifty or sixty sailors on the street in front of the Bucket O' Blood. When they heard *monkeys* they started laughing and cheering.

Monica had no idea what was going on, laughing and hanging on her swabby. He pulled her close and leaned back against the rock wall by the Bucket. He pointed at us and said something and his friends laughed. The crowd started talking loud again, turning their backs on us.

"Don't *move*!" Booley spit to CC. "That's guy's *mines*!"

For a minute I thought, Lift up your shirt, CC, and show those bigmouths what you got hiding under there. Then I woke up. What am I *saying*?

Booley walked to the edge of the street. "Eh, you," he yelled to Monica's guy.

The whole crowd turned around, and Booley said, "Not all you stupits, just that one. You. Yeah, you. Come in the street and face me, man to man. . . . Oh, excuse me, you are a man, yeah? Hard to tell."

Everybody looked at the sailor. He wasn't laughing anymore.

CHAPTER 20

The sailor shoved Monica away. She stumbled, but another man caught her and helped her back up. When CC saw that, he blasted into the street and almost got hit by a car, brakes screeching, driver honking, *Blat! Blat! Blat! Blat!*

Booley ran after him and grabbed his shirt. "He's *mines*, I told you!"

Booley let go of CC and turned back to the swabby, who was handing his hat and wallet to his friend.

I checked the pier. Rocky and Sergeant were still there, lights flashing.

Turning back, I saw Leonard, looking jumpy, waiting for somebody to move, somebody who wasn't that one guy Booley was going after. He would hold back until Booley creamed the guy, or shamed himself. Leonard was there to see Booley lose his rep. Vulture.

"Yo, monkey," the Navy guy called to Booley. He thumbed in Monica's direction. "Did this used to be your girlfriend?"

When Booley took a step forward, the sailor turned around and pulled Monica up to him and kissed her right on the mouth. Then he looked back at Booley and licked his lips. "Ummm." Man, I thought CC would pull that gun and kill the guy right then and there. But somehow he didn't.

Me? I couldn't *breathe*.

Booley said, "Come fight, big mout'. I take you right here in the middle of this street. Let's go."

The guy in the car backed up, slowly. No more honking.

The swabby let Monica go and pushed through the crowd to the street. Monica looked dazed as Janet pulled her arm to leave. *Run*, I begged Monica. *You can get away now.* But she just stood there looking confused.

The sailor came up to Booley and shoved him, a small push.

We shot off that wall like wild dogs and closed in around Booley. My heart was pounding, *bu-bum*, *bu-*

bum, let's go, let's go. Ten, twenty, thirty swabbys shouting at us, smacking their hands with their fists.

"I'm only gonna say this once," the milk bottle said to Booley. "You start something with me, you better be able to finish it, boy, because I aim to tear your head off if you do."

Bok! Booley popped him.

The sailor staggered back, put his hand on his nose and bent over, blood in his hand. Then the guy looked up at Booley. And *smiled.* He said, "Bad choice, black boy."

He came at Booley, fat fists flying. But Booley slipped away using strokes and moves like karate or aikido or judo. The swabby was getting red-face because he couldn't connect. Booley whopped the guy in the stomach with his foot. *Fop!* Like a foot boxer. *Fop! Fop!* The swabby grunted and stumbled, then came back harder, swinging and missing. Booley was good, man. Dodging and moving around like a real street fighter. He wasn't about to lose no rep tonight.

Hoo, the swabby's face was red. He charged Booley again. *Bonk!* One solid slug in Booley's stomach. Booley staggered back, hit the road gasping.

The Navy guys all yelling, *Get him! Get him!* The crowd in the Bucket O' Blood poured out, so now it was like a hundred of them to one of us. My hands were shaking bad, but I felt strong, ready.

The guy jumped on top of Booley and smashed his face again and again while Booley's arms were pinned under the guy's legs. *Whap! Whap! Whap!*

CC charged the swabby and took him down.

And that was it.

All of us guys poured out into the street, the Navy guys swarming over us, punching, punching. Leonard and his snakes went to work around me. Grunting, shouting. *Whop! Bam! Bok! Ooof!* Kalani and Reggie were somewhere nearby. I could hear them yelling. Seemed like the whole world was fighting. Then I was looking in some guy's face. He looked young as me. I tried to pop his nose, but missed. My fist slammed his cheek. He blinked, shook his head to clear it. *Bok!* He ground his knuckles into my eye.

A sharp pain shot back. White explosions popped in my head. He hit me again and I went down. Some swabby's shoe squashed my arm. Another foot stood on my chest. Somebody tripped and fell on me. I rolled up to protect myself. The street was hard and rough under my face. Small rocks, flattened gum. Smelled like gas. Tasted like blood. All the time above me was men growling and slugging like sharks in a feeding frenzy, snapping at your head, your feet, your throat. Then somebody yelled, *"He's got a gun!"*

Like roaches, everybody ran. Even me, crawling on my hands and knees to the side of the road. Trying to see, trying to focus. And then I saw him.

Booley.

Alone in the street, staggering, shaking his head, blinking.

CC stood nearby, the .38 in his hand. *No, no, no!* "*Booley!*" CC yelled.

Booley looked up just as CC tossed him the gun. He almost dropped it, but caught it and looked at it, still blinking, now holding the gun by the grip.

A sailor charged him to try and take the gun away, but Booley brought it up and the Navy guy ran back.

Booley looked stunned, like he didn't know what to do with a gun in his hand. He swung it around, swabbys scrambling for cover. The ones who came out from the Bucket now crammed back inside.

Leonard and his snakes were backing off. I ran to the seawall. Only Booley was in the street, still blinking and squinting, waving that gun back and forth at the ducking shapes around him. The swabby who started the whole thing was standing right there by him, and Booley didn't even know it.

Lights coming, flashing blue. Screeching tires.

Rocky.

I faded back, Kalani and Reggie moving with me.

Rocky shoved his way through the crowd, pulling out his gun. Leonard and his snakes ran. Then me, Reggie, and Kalani ran, me all the time thinking, *No, we gotta stay, gotta help Booley!* But we didn't.

I heard Rocky yell and I stopped to look back.

"Drop the gun!" Rocky shouted. *"Drop it or I going shoot! Drop it now!"*

Booley, looking over his shoulder, turned to where he heard Rocky's voice. He aimed that gun at Rocky and Rocky fired.

Pop!

Booley jerked back.

Blam! Uncle Randy's .38 went off. The bullet smashed a window at the ABC store. Navy guys hit the street. Booley went down. The .38 flew out of his hand and clinked across the road toward the curb. A swabby picked it up and held it nose-down.

Rocky ran to Booley, who was squirming and holding his leg. *"Ahhh,"* Booley yelled, *"ahhhh,"* his mouth all twisted.

Rocky put his gun away, kneeling down next to Booley. "Somebody call an ambulance!"

Kalani and Reggie took off. Then me. Cowards.

Two SPs sprinted past us, then Sergeant Tiumalu's car came squealing by. We dropped down to hide, then got up and ran out to the end of the pier. I was dizzy. Stars popping in my eyes. I glanced back at the crowd now coming out of the Bucket to gape at Booley. Some sailors were still fighting with CC.

Another police car screeched up, blue lights whirling.

Daddy jumped out, with his shotgun.

CHAPTER 21

*B*laammm!

One monster blast in the air. The crackling echo shot across the water. Guys hit the ground. CC ran into an alley and vanished. Daddy watched him, the shotgun pointing up.

My hands were shaking like crazy.

"Let's *go!*" Reggie said.

"Swim," Kalani said. "Jump in and swim to Kona Inn, then get out there and go down to my place."

"But then we going get wet," Reggie said.

"Get wet or get arrested."

All the time everything was going down,

Olomana was playing at King Kam. Prob'ly nobody even heard those gunshots.

We crept over to the edge of the pier. The water was black. Out in the bay ghost boats slept by gray buoys. A siren sounded, coming louder. I could see men moving away as an ambulance crept through them, flashing red light on the buildings.

Kalani jumped in the water. Then me.

"I don't believe this," Reggie said, and followed us.

The ocean was warm and salty and smelled like boat fuel. We were down so low now that I couldn't see what was going on over the seawall. The water swirled around my neck. Seemed like a week since this morning when I was swimming by my house, working out. All I wanted from this day was to check out a destroyer and watch a fight.

Booley, I thought. *Please be all right. Please!*

Kalani went the long way, swimming past Kona Inn and around the point into the small bay on the other side. Took about twenty minutes. We got out by his house, climbing up on the rocks and creeping through the weeds to the street. We stood on the road in the dark, squeezing water out of our T-shirts. A car came by, but we were too tired to hide, so we just turned our backs to it.

At Kalani's place Sergeant Tiumalu's car was in the yard.

We backed into the bushes.

"Now what?" Reggie whispered.

"Maybe he's looking for my old man," Kalani said.

"I don't think so."

"Let's hide at the cemetery," I said. "Nobody going look there."

"Are you crazy?" Reggie said. "At night?"

"Nobody will check it, I tell you."

"Mokes is right," Kalani said. "You rather go to jail?"

Must have been about eleven o'clock by then. Pretty soon the Navy guys would be heading back to their ship.

We crept past the Catholic church and up into the cemetery behind it. I could hear the soft rumble of waves breaking on the rocky shore, and somebody's dog barking. It wouldn't stop. The shadowy lines of gravestones made me think of Night Marchers, and I prayed I wouldn't hear flutes, or drums, or somebody whispering my name. Bad thoughts, like ants, crawled in my mind, thoughts about swimming with sharks, about Monica, CC, and Uncle Randy's .38. But one especially ugly one came pushing up: for the first time in my life I was on the other side of Daddy. It made me sick. It made me want to lie facedown in the dirt with no clothes on, and beg all those bad spirits to go somewheres else.

"This is crazy," Reggie said after only a few minutes of hiding. He stood up. "I'm going home, already. See you guys tomorrow."

"Ain't going be no tomorrow," I mumbled.

Something like a mongoose or a cat rustled through the weeds and nearly gave Reggie a heart attack. "I *hate* this place," he said.

Kalani and I watched him pick his way up the hill, stepping over gravestones, careful not to tread on dead bones and rotting faces. "Sergeant going get us sooner or later," I said to Kalani. "Might as well just go wait at your house."

We were back out on the street in less than a minute.

Sergeant Tiumalu was gone now, and Kalani's house was black and quiet. Except for that dumb dog. "Shaddup!" Kalani yelled, and Bozo started whining.

Inside Kalani's room we kept the light off. I sat down on the floor and Kalani went over to his creaky bed. Where was Booley now? At the hospital? In jail? In a coffin?

Headlights flashed across Kalani's wall and I stood up. "He's back," I whispered.

But it wasn't Sergeant Tiumalu.

CHAPTER 22

We kept quiet, pretending to sleep.

Outside, I could hear Daddy's police radio spitting. The car door thumped shut. Bozo started barking, then growling, then whining, then he went quiet. Just like Daddy to shut him up easy.

A knock at the door.

Kalani messed up his hair, made a sleepy face. I took off my shirt, like how I sleep at home. I looked at Kalani, then we headed out to open the door. Just maybe Daddy didn't hear we were there. And maybe he never saw that .38. Maybe they really were looking for Kalani's old man.

You dreaming, boy.

When Kalani opened the door, Daddy didn't look at me. "Your father home, Kalani?"

"N-No."

"Leave him a note, then. Tell him he can find you by calling the police station." For a second Kalani stared at Daddy. *What?*

"Hurry it up," Daddy said.

"Daddy," I said, but he put up his hand to hush me.

I looked down at my feet and waited.

Kalani finished the note and said, "Okay."

"You boys come with me."

When we walked out to the police car Bozo whined at Kalani, but Kalani ignored him. Daddy still wouldn't look at me, would hardly look at Kalani. He opened the back door. "Get in," he said to me. "You, get in front," he told Kalani.

I bent down to get in, but stopped. Someone else was already in the car.

Monica, eyes glassy with tears, looked up at me. Janet was on the other side, staring at the seat in front of her.

Slowly, I got in.

The second I brushed up against Monica, she grabbed my hand and squeezed so hard I heard my knuckles crack. I wanted to say something, to help her somehow, to comfort her.

Daddy got in and slammed the door, then started the car.

Monica smelled like old perfume, booze, and cigarette smoke. She sobbed, but silently, resting her head on my shoulder, gripping my hand.

Daddy drove us into town and stopped in front of the Bucket O' Blood. Only a few sailors were there now, all of them inside. But across the harbor, in the faint light on the pier, I could see fifty or sixty of them standing around waiting for the launch to come back from the ship.

Daddy took a long look in the bar, then drove us down to the pier.

When we circled out onto it, I pulled Monica closer so no one could see her when we passed the crowd of sailors. My shirt was getting wet from her tears. Janet stroked Monica's hair, saying nothing. Daddy turned the car around and drove back through town one more time. The place was quiet.

We drove along the coast road, past Kalani's house, past my house, down to almost the end of the road where Monica lived. I had my arm around her now, not feeling at all like any kind of lover boy.

When Daddy pulled up to Monica's place she tried to disappear, shrinking down between my shoulder and the seat.

A light went on in the dark house. Her daddy opened the screen door, squinting into the headlights. He held up his hand to block the brightness. "Is that you, Jimmy?"

Daddy got out without answering, opened the back door on Janet's side. Janet got out.

"She's okay, Gilbert," Daddy finally said. "Sometime tomorrow afternoon I'll come out and we can talk about what happened tonight."

Monica's daddy bent down and peeked into the car, a deep frown carved on his face. Monica wouldn't look at him, and wouldn't get out.

Daddy leaned in and put a hand around Monica's arm. "Let's go," he said gently. But she wouldn't budge.

"I'll get her out," her father said.

"No you won't," Monica's moms said, pushing him out of the way. "Come, baby, come inside."

The daddy backed off, mumbling.

"Go on," I whispered. "It's okay. It's your moms."

Monica sat up and wiped her eyes, then slowly got out.

When we got to Janet's house, Daddy let her out and said, "Tell Reggie to come out. Dressed. He's coming with me."

Janet nodded and went in.

A couple minutes later Reggie came out scowling, like he thought maybe me and Kalani turned him in. Daddy held the door open. Reggie slid in next to me. He didn't say a word. And neither did I.

Daddy drove away fast, taking us somewhere,

prob'ly to jail. Nobody talked. There was only Daddy's radio making static. If it was jail, then I didn't mind. Anything would be better than how Daddy wasn't talking to me, or even looking at me.

But jail is not where we went.

CHAPTER 23

Daddy parked at the hospital emergency entrance and got out and opened my door. We followed him inside. The nurse on duty said, "Room 135."

Rocky Machado was sitting on a metal chair by the door to room 135 looking kind of sick. He stood up when he saw us.

"How's he doing?" Daddy asked.

Rocky shook his head. "Okay, I guess. Prob'ly have a permanent limp. I didn't want to shoot him, Chief. I—"

"S'okay, Rocky," Daddy said. "You were doing your job."

Rocky looked at the floor and nodded.

Daddy said to Rocky, "Go home. I'll take it from here, but first thing tomorrow see if you can find CC. I want to talk to him."

"He's not going anywhere, Chief."

Except to maybe jail, I thought.

Daddy went into the room. Me, Kalani, and Reggie followed.

There was Booley, his leg and his head wrapped up in bandages. A plastic bag of clear liquid hung from a silver pole with a tube running down to a piece of tape on his arm. At first Booley looked dead. But when I got closer he cracked one eye open, the one that wasn't swollen shut.

"Aay . . . cockaroach," he whispered.

I stared at Booley. Kalani and Reggie were somewhere behind me, keeping quiet. I couldn't think of what to say.

"How's the leg?" Daddy asked.

"Fine. I can't feel anything."

Daddy bunched his lips. "Dammit, Booley, since when did you start messing with guns? Rocky could have killed you."

Booley turned toward the moths crowding the black window screen.

Then, for the first time, Daddy looked at me. "How'd he get the .38, Eric?"

"I—"

"Wasn't him," Booley said, still looking away. He spoke so softly, I almost couldn't hear him. "I took it from your house. Mokes didn't know."

I looked at Booley's arm, where the tube was going in. I couldn't look at his face, or Daddy's. I couldn't look at anybody. It was just like Booley to take the rap for CC. Never rat on your friends. Stand by them no matter what. Yeah. Like how I stood by Booley when CC threw him that gun.

"Mokes," Booley whispered.

I looked up.

"Scare me."

"What?"

"*Scare* me."

Talking crazy now. I looked at Daddy, but Daddy's face said nothing.

I turned back to Booley. "I . . . I don't know what you mean."

"Just do it . . . scare me."

"*Yaaahh!*" I said, making a quick move.

Booley flinched. "Can you see me?" he said.

"Yeah."

"Good. I'm not a ghost yet."

"You not a ghost, Booley."

He closed his one eye. "I'm not ready to be dead."

I looked at him lying there with closed eyes. Sissy came to mind. And Granma.

"Eh, Mokes. You know what's my family's aumakua? Shark."

"Shark?"

Still with his eyes closed, Booley said softly, "I going adopt you, punk. From now on no shark going hurt you. They going protect you."

Must be the pain pills. I reached to touch his shoulder but stopped when Daddy said, "Go sit in the car, son. All three of you."

We started to go, but Booley said, "One more thing, Mokes."

Daddy's face said, Okay, but hurry it up.

"Over there by the closet," Booley said. "Inside that paper bag got my clothes."

I got the bag and peeked in at his bloodstained shorts and T-shirt.

"In the back pocket. Take it to Granma for me, okay?"

A folded-up piece of paper. His paycheck from the *Captain Cook*, signed on the back to Granma.

Daddy drove me, Kalani, and Reggie back down to Kailua.

It was one-thirty on Daddy's clock by the time we stopped at Kalani's house. When Kalani saw a light on inside his face got sour. I prayed for Kalani's sake that his old man was too drunk to remember what happened on the pier.

"You meet me down at the Bucket O' Blood to-morrow morning at ten o'clock," Daddy said to Kalani after he let him out.

"The Bucket O' Blood?"

"Ten o'clock. Is that clear?"

"Yeah."

Kalani went in and we drove off, me and Reggie in the backseat. "You two be there too," Daddy said into the rearview mirror. "Ten o'clock." And those were the last words he said that night.

We dropped Reggie off and headed home.

Daddy pulled up in front of our house and got out. He slammed his door, opened mine, and went inside the house.

I stayed in the car, thinking, looking at the ocean, so smooth and dark. Almost black. But I could still see it.

After a few minutes I got out and went down by the rocks. You so damn stupit, Mokes. So damn stupit. Look how bad you screwed up today. Only this morning Daddy put his hand on your face and said, "I love you, son." And now he's looking at you like you're nothing.

I sat down on a flat rock as close to the ocean as I could get. The waves were low and soft. Thumping, hissing. I thought about Booley, about him lying in the hospital, alone. No moms, no dad. Nobody there with him except maybe a nurse.

Then I remembered a long time back. It was one

morning about a month after Booley's old man died. I found Booley sitting here on these same rocks where I was now, right in front of our house. Daddy had already gone to the station and Moms was just starting work in her shed when I first spotted him. It was weird. This was before Daddy made him come to talk. Booley just came on his own, I guess because he knew me and Daddy pretty good by then.

Anyways, I watched him a while; then, when he didn't leave, I went out to see what he was doing.

"Booley," I called as I came up behind him. "It's me, Mokes."

He didn't turn around, didn't answer.

I sat down next to him. "What you doing here?"

Still silent. I waited. His eyes were kind of glazed, like he was in deep thought about something. The ocean was nice that morning, calm and fresh. Two deep-sea charter boats trolled the horizon, white dots on a blue sea. I remember them because it was such a strange morning, finding Booley Domingo sitting in front of my house.

Finally, Booley said, "I came to see the chief . . . but his car was gone."

"I can call him," I said. "He'll come home."

"No . . . no . . . forget it. I . . ."

And that's when Booley broke down. Cried and cried and cried. Scared me, I tell you. With his face in his hands he sobbed, two, three minutes. Then he stopped and wiped the tears from his face. He looked back out to sea, not seeming embarrassed about it.

"What is it, Boo? What's the matter?"

He shook his head, like saying, Forget it, I don't want to talk about it. But then he said, "I just wanted to talk to your old man."

I waited for more. Picked up a rock and felt its weight in my hand. Put it back down. Waited. Let him take his time.

Five, six minutes later Booley stood up and gave me a glare. "You tell anyone you saw me like this, Mokes, and you going be real sorry."

"No, no, I not going tell, don't worry."

"That's good, Mokes," he said. He looked at his feet a moment, like he was thinking of how to get out of there with face. I tried to make it easy for him. "You were never here, Booley. I never saw you today, yeah?"

He smiled, kind of shy, which you hardly ever saw in Booley Domingo. "Yeah, I gone, already." And he left.

I never told anyone about that, even though maybe I should have told Daddy. But Booley said not to tell, so I didn't. For days I thought about why he wanted to talk to Daddy and I finally decided that it was because of maybe a couple things, but mostly one: that Daddy would listen. After his father died Booley had to worry about Sissy too. He had nobody to turn to and was prob'ly scared. And that's what I decided: Booley Domingo was scared.

Not long after that Booley changed. He got angry. He started spending more time with guys like CC. He made a tattoo on his hand, a homemade one that said *Death*.

CHAPTER 24

Next morning I jumped awake.

Already nine-thirty. Aw, man. *Nine-thirty.* I lay back down and covered my eyes. First time this summer I missed my workout. But I was tired. Man, was I tired.

After five minutes I got up and looked out the window. Daddy's car was gone. There was only the empty yard and the smooth and perfect ocean. I could almost feel myself diving in. But today that wouldn't happen.

When Moms saw me coming out from my room she tried to smile. But then she said, "Why did you lie to us, Eric? Why?"

I just shrugged. I didn't *know* why.

"You hurt Daddy, you know. He trusted you. He didn't say five words to me this morning." Moms went over to the shelf and took down a box of Grape-Nuts. "You better eat something before you go."

I stared at the box. How could I eat? Even if I was starving, how could I eat? "Moms," I said. "Moms . . ."

She looked down, shook her head.

I went outside, shutting the door easy.

Quiet. No birds, no waves.

The wood steps were nice and warm under my feet. Ehu, lounging on the bottom step, got up and stretched. No wind, no clouds. Just sunny and peaceful and perfect and would prob'ly be the worst day of my life.

The road was so hot, I had to walk on the white lines or else fry my feet. My eye hurt when I touched it. I forgot to look in the mirror to see if it was black-and-blue.

The town seemed kind of strange now, like how you feel when somebody just told you somebody you know died. I wondered if today Booley could feel his leg, and what it was like to have a bullet hole in your body.

When I got to Kalani's house I checked the yard, but didn't go down to see if he was home. I only had fifteen minutes to get to the Bucket O' Blood, and no way was I going to be late. Anyway, Kalani was prob'ly already gone. If his old man hadn't killed him.

There were a few tourists out on the street, shopping and looking around. But the town was quiet and still and lazy as always. There was the big banyan tree by the Palace, with a couple thousand mynah birds screeching away in it. And by the church across the street, two lovers were holding hands and reading the brass sign that told about when it was built. Then there was the small beach where the seawall starts, its water clear and sandy green.

Looked just like any other day.

I jumped up on the seawall and thought, *the destroyer!*

But the horizon was sharp and clear.

Gone.

When I got down by the Bucket O' Blood, Kalani and Reggie were sitting on the curb in front of the saloon. They sat a few feet away from each other, Kalani with his elbows on his knees, and Reggie leaning back on his hands. Kalani looked over at me and raised his chin, *hello.* I jumped off the seawall and walked over.

The Bucket was closed and empty. It had that sweet stink of spilled beer. The bruise on Kalani's cheek and his purple-colored eye made me wince.

Was it from his daddy or the street fight? I wondered if I looked that bad. "Howzit?" I said.

"Not too good, I guess," Kalani said. "Where's your daddy? How come you didn't come with him?"

"He ain't talking to me."

Kalani nodded. "What he going do with us?"

I shrugged. "Send us to Alcatraz?"

Reggie snickered, but Kalani didn't. He threw a pebble out toward the ocean. I stood looking down at him. "Did your old man give you that black eye?"

Kalani shook his head no. "I found him sitting on the porch at six o'clock this morning. Had tearstains on his dirty face. I asked if he was okay, but it was like he couldn't hear me, or like he was on another planet, you know? So I sat down next to him and waited."

"Was he drunk?"

"No, was more like he was all fought out, you know?"

"He got into a fight?"

"Only in his head, I guess. He sat there about ten minutes." Kalani looked at his cut-up hand, the one his old man mangled. "Then he grabbed my hand and checked out these cuts he made with that stick on the pier last night. His fingers were so dirty I thought they would give me an infection, so I pulled my hand away." Kalani paused a moment, then added, "After a while he went in the house. Never said nothing. That's all."

"Weird, man."

Kalani threw another pebble. "Look. They gone."

I gazed out toward the empty ocean. "You know, if Daddy wanted to arrest us, he would have done it last night."

"What could he arrest us for?" Reggie said. "We didn't do anything."

"We knew about that gun."

"So?"

I sat down between Reggie and Kalani, but we didn't talk.

At ten o'clock sharp Daddy drove up. He stopped and sat in his car a minute, writing something. He parked in front of the fire hydrant. Cops don't even notice things like that. They would park on the side-walk if they wanted to.

Finally, Daddy got out.

Kalani, Reggie, and I stood up. I rubbed my chin. Kalani put his hands in his pockets, his gaze fixed on some spot on the ground. Reggie scowled.

Daddy walked around the back of the car, pulling up his pants. "Follow me," he said, his eyes looking tired. Prob'ly slept only a couple hours.

He stepped out into the street. A car was coming. It slowed down, but Daddy waved it past, then walked out in the street and stopped. He pointed to the road. "Burn this into your brains."

Me, Kalani, and Reggie looked down at the blacktop at a blackish red stain, about as big as my hand spread open. Booley's blood.

"When you mess with guns you can die," Daddy said. "Any other police officer would not have taken the chance Rocky took. He would have shot to kill. And Booley would be dead."

I stared at the bloodstain. I didn't have to burn it into my brain. It was in there forever.

Another car came, but Daddy didn't move. The car stopped and waited.

"Reach down and touch that spot," Daddy said. "Store that bloody stain in your memory."

We knelt down and touched it with the tips of our fingers.

"Put your whole hand down on top of it," Daddy commanded, and we did. Already the street was hot. Bloody and hot.

When I got up I wiped my hand on my shorts and looked into Daddy's eyes. *Daddy, I . . . Daddy . . .*

Kalani and Reggie just stood there looking down at the stain.

Daddy peeked back at the waiting car, then put his hands on our shoulders and walked us to the side of the road.

As the car drove by, Daddy said, "You boys think guns and fighting and acting tough gives you respect, don't you? You think pushing people around gives you some kind of power."

Kalani and Reggie still looked down, their heads bowed like in church. I thought, Well, yeah. Look at Booley. Look at CC.

"Those things only make people afraid of you, and fear is not respect. What people respect you for is not this," he said, making a fist. Then he tapped his heart and said, "It's this."

Kalani's eyebrows were jammed together in a frown, thinking. Reggie still scowled, only now his scowl looked kind of sad. But me, I was feeling the weight of Daddy's hand on my shoulder. It felt good to have it there, so good I can't even describe it.

"I haven't told your mother everything, Mokes," Daddy said. "But when I do . . . it's going to scare her."

I felt like I had a stone caught in my throat.

Nobody talked. What was there to say?

"Okay," Daddy said, kind of sighing. "You boys can go."

Go? But . . .

Kalani and Reggie started to walk away.

"Wait," I said, and they stopped.

I turned to face Daddy. To face the badge, the uniform. *So* hard to look at him. But I had to, even though I knew that now he must respect me about as much as some criminal. I blinked a couple times when I thought of that.

But Booley and CC . . . everybody looks up to them. Nobody messes with them. Daddy was wrong. He just didn't know what it was like. He just didn't . . . just didn't . . .

No.

I blinked again, but still looked straight at Daddy.

How could you respect somebody who let a friend down? And when I let CC keep that gun that's just what I did. Let Booley down. I was too chicken to keep fighting until I got it back.

I couldn't look at Daddy's eyes one more second, and I couldn't think of any words to say. So I did the only thing left to do, even though Kalani and Reggie were watching. I went up to Daddy and hugged him. I'm sorry, Daddy. I'm sorry.

And he hugged me back.

So hard I couldn't breathe.

Author's Note:

As I meet readers all over the continental United States, I am constantly being asked to pronounce the unusual words and character names that inevitably pop up in my fiction. I hope this helps. Look me up at http://www.bdd.com/teachers for a spoken version of this pronunciation guide and lots of other good stuff.

Aumakua	ow· ma· ku· ah
Booley	boo· lee
Ehu	eh· hoo
Haole	how· lay
Hinalea	hee· na· lay· ah
Imu	ee· moo
Kailua	kai· loo· ah
Kainaliu	kai· na· lee· oo
Kalani	ka· la· nee
Kealakekua	kay· ah· la· kay· koo· ah
Keauhou	kay· ow· ho
Keoni	kay· oh· nee
Konawaena	ko· na· why· na
Kuamoʻo	koo· ah· mo· oh
Kukae	koo· kai
Mokes	moeks
Obake	oh· ba· kay
Olomana	oh· lo· ma· na
Shaka	sha· ka
Shi-shi	shee· shee
Tiumalu	tee· oo· ma· loo
Uhane	oo· ha· nay

Aloha,

Graham Salisbury